Her Heart's Secret

by

Janet Nitsick

Her Heart's Secret

Janet Syas Nitsick

Chapter One

Erina placed her exercise book, slate and her lunch, wrapped in an old newspaper, into her chocolate-brown leather satchel then fastened it. She shook her head and yelled, "Ma, I'm leaving."

Her mother rushed into the kitchen. "I'm sorry, Erina. I needed to help your brother get dressed." She studied her daughter, the braided auburn pigtails resting on her shoulders and the two missing upper teeth. "You got everything? Your lunch? Your books?"

"Yes, I'm all set." Erina took a deep breath to calm her queasy stomach. She hated to lie to her mother, but she could not tell her how nervous she was about going to a new school.

Ma hugged her daughter before stepping back. Ma examined Erina. "You look good in peach."

"Thank you for the cotton dress you sized down for me."

"Yes, it fits and the rip near the hem doesn't show," added her ma.

Erina wanted to assure her mother, but she knew when she sat, the rip would show. The hole was too big to fix. Erina just hoped no one at her new school would notice. She clamped her lips together.

"It's all right to be worried about your first day. I'm sure there are other eight-year-olds." Her mother's voice broke. "Your father and I had to move here, or we'd have nothing. We've got to be thankful Pa's father left this farm, so we could make a new start."

"Yes, Ma." Erina fought back the tears as she thought of the big house they had left back East to come here. "Well, I'd better go."

Her mother adjusted her daughter's white collar before she pressed her daughter to her for a minute. "Everything will be fine. You'll see."

Erina nodded before she hung the satchel's strap over her left shoulder and dashed out the door. She inhaled a long breath in the hopes of preventing the streams of held-back tears from falling. However, they came anyway like river rapids rushing over rocks.

She wiped her face with her palms before she glanced at the weather-beaten house where they now lived. Weeds marked the house's front. She closed her wet eyelashes a second to remember the abundant flower beds edged with ruby-red and pale-pink roses around their former large home back East.

The chickens clucked and the cow mooed as Erina eased her way down the hill, making sure each step she took was secure. The last thing she needed was to fall in this wet brown grass and get her dress dirty. She maneuvered around a tall weed. Her foot slipped. but she steadied herself, thanks to her high-topped black ankle boots. *Good boots. You've been with me through thick and thin.*

She laughed, but as she did so, a tear streaked down her cheek. Taking her left two fingers, she wiped away the teardrop. She clamped her lips together, knowing they could never return to the house back East. Erina inhaled then exhaled a long breath before she continued down the gradual slope.

At the hill's bottom, she stood still several seconds while she gazed at the schoolhouse ahead of her. She gulped at seeing the small, white-painted structure. Her lips trembled. How could she go to such a poorly constructed place? She squeezed her eyelids together, and her mind took her back to the school she attended last year. She sighed, remembering the large schoolhouse with its lattice windows and its double-door entrance.

The school bell rang.

Erina pried her eyelids open and clamped her lips together as she dashed toward the schoolhouse. Her feet creaked on the entrance's wooden planks. She was about to open the door when a tall, slender boy, who wore tan trousers rolled up above his ankles, bumped into her as he grabbed the door's handle.

"Excuse me. I'm late!" He tipped his mangled hat to Erina before he returned it to his head. He jerked the door open. "Women first." He crooked a smile. "Or should I say little girls first? We're late. Miss Clarke doesn't cotton to tardiness."

Erina gulped, knowing tardiness was no way to begin her first school day.

* * *

They entered and stepped to the back of the room. Adam, 11, crooked his head downward to the cute little stranger with freckled cheeks and braided pigtails. "You've got to take a seat."

"But—but where?" she mumbled.

"There." He pointed to several girls who sat upfront on a long wooden plank. She hesitated. He cleared his throat and whispered, "You've got to move, or we'll be in trouble." Adam grabbed her hand before letting go of it. "Go, sit by the little girl wearing that big white apron. She's the preacher's daughter."

Erina nodded and maneuvered forward.

Miss Clarke, who had been writing letters on the long blackboard upfront, turned around to see the new pupil scoot beside Bertha.

Adam inched himself to a rear seat where the boys sat. As he wiggled onto the plank, the wood creaked.

Miss Clarke shifted her gaze from the girl to Adam. The teacher glared at him. "Adam, see me after the opening."

Adam's stomach churned. *That little girl got me in this mess. Now Miss Clarke knows I was late. Way to go, whomever you are!*

Miss Clarke rang her teacher's bell. The pupils rose. The boys bowed then the girls curtsied. "Sit down and we'll begin the day with a scripture reading from Proverbs 11:

'Even a child is known by his doings, whether his work *be* pure, or whether *it be* right.'"

Miss Clarke cleared her throat and said, "So I expect everyone to pay attention and not doodle around." She turned to the new girl. "I see we have a new pupil. Please stand and introduce yourself."

The sheepish little girl, in a peach dress, stood up as her shoulders shook. Face flushed, she stammered out in a New England accent, "My name is Erina Higgins."

The boys snickered. Adam glared at Clarence, the boy who started the laughter.

Clarence glimpsed at Adam before he slumped in his seat.

Adam shook his head and glared at his classmate. *Good. Glad you got the message. She did not deserve your disrespect.* He returned his gaze to Miss Clarke.

The teacher shifted her gaze from one boy to the other, settling on Adam.

I didn't make fun of her. I didn't. I didn't. He gulped. His stomach tensed.

"I'm sorry for the boys' behavior. They shouldn't make fun of your brogue. We're not accustomed to that accent here, but we'll get used to it." The teacher shifted her gaze to each of the eight boys before settling her gaze on Adam.

I know I'm usually the troublemaker, but this time it wasn't me. I didn't do it! Adam swallowed the lump in his throat.

Miss Clarke broke her gaze then gave Erina a small smile. "You know how to read?"

"Yes, Miss Clarke," Erina said in a weak voice.

"Then Bertha, share your book with Erina and read the play, 'The Simpleton.' If weather is good, we'll act this out Wednesday with the older boys playing Simpleton, the king and the servants. Adam and Erina will be the farmers."

Erina's countenance paled.

"Oh, no!" Adam uttered under his breath. He clamped his teeth together.

"Adam, come here!"

Taking a deep breath, he stared at the new girl as he passed her to stand in front of the teacher. "Yes, Miss Clarke."

"You know the rules, and how I don't appreciate your continued tardiness. I'll not have this year start out like last year. So, you sit in that Dunce's chair and wear the Dunce hat. Perhaps you'll realize you must be on time."

He maneuvered to the corner chair, picked up the coned hat and placed it on his head. Then he wormed his body onto the high seat. He glared at the cute foreign girl. *You. You're the one who caused me all this trouble. If only you had taken a seat right away, I wouldn't have gotten caught.*

Chapter Two

Twelve Years Later, 1891
Tekamah, Nebraska

The early spring breeze rustled against Erina's long skirt as she stooped to pick the array of colorful tulips from rose red to white linen and bright yellow, which graced the front of her deceased parents' home. She had returned to her house of discontent to bury her mother. Erina planned to place her ma's grave next to her pa in Mount Calvary Lutheran's cemetery.

The cemetery was located behind the white church with its tall steeple. Today, she would decorate the parlor with these gorgeous blooms as her mother's body lay in the wooden casket, made by her brother. The parson would officiate the short ceremony, and neighbors and friends would come to express their condolences. A tear fell onto the spattering of tulips she held in her hand. *Oh Ma, I didn't mean to leave you alone like this. I should've stayed and taken care of you instead of accepting that teaching position in Blair.*

I know you insisted I take it, but leaving you all by yourself wasn't right. Of course, her brother, Lee, was here, but boys never were good at taking care of others, especially him since his wife ruled him like a queen's subject.

Erina wrapped her hand around the bouquet as the damp leaves and blooms caressed her fingers. She rushed toward the house, opened the small door, and stepped to the china cabinet to reach for the tall glass vase inside. Going to the kitchen, she cut the stems, pumped water into the vase, then added the flowers.

She examined the pretty blooms. Ma would have loved this. She always tried to perk up the house with flowers. Erina released a long breath. Flowers had made her ma remember the beautiful bouquets scattered throughout their big house back East. *That's where everyone was merry, even me.*

Erina shook her head. *You can't go back. We've tried to make the best of this dilapidated place, but you can't drown out the happiness we had there.* She bit her lower lip, took a deep breath and entered the parlor.

The casket sat in the middle of the room. Erina set the bouquet on the small table underneath the wide window with lace curtains. She backed away. *Yes, Ma would love this.*

Clasping her hands together, she pressed them under her chin, looked at her ma then stepped to the bedroom to put on her funeral attire.

* * *

Erina pulled her high-necked creamed-colored crepe bodice over her head before sliding the mother-of-pearl buttons into the homemade buttonholes. Slipping the midnight black skirt over her head, she fastened the waistband. The full skirt fell around her ankles. She reached for the small black hat, which she placed upon her pinned-up hair.

Normally, she would look into her dresser's mirror to check her appearance; however, it now was covered with black fabric to prevent her from looking into it, which would prevent her mother from going to heaven.

From her dresser drawer, Erina reached for her laced handkerchief. She would need one today. She closed the bedroom door then stepped toward the parlor. Her brother rushed into the room.

Lee turned to his sister. "Do you need any help?"

"No, everything is ready for the visitors. I picked some tulips to make the room nice and, of course, it's something Ma would've loved."

"Yes, she would've."

"Thanks also for hanging the black crepe above the front door." Her throat constricted. "Oh no! I forgot to stop the windup clock. I've got to do that, or we'll have bad luck, and we can't have that today."

Lee's wife, Mary, stepped closer. "Don't worry; we'll do that. You go and rest, and we'll sit with Ma for a time. Have you had something to eat?"

Erina shook her head. Tears pulled at her eyelids. She had been preparing the house and just now realized how worn out she was. "Thank you," she wheezed. "I forgot all about eating. Neighbors brought over nuts, cheese, raisins and an apple pie."

Lee reached out his hand to his sister and held it several seconds before he turned to his wife and headed for the parlor.

Grateful her brother and sister-in-law were there, Erina maneuvered her tired frame toward the dining room and kitchen. She plopped down in a dining-room chair. *These boots hurt!* She sighed then slipped off her knee-high, white-and-black leather boots then peeled off her socks. Free at last. She wiggled her sore toes. Her stomach grumbled. *I've got to get something to eat.* Barefoot and unladylike, she labored to the kitchen.

* * *

She munched on the walnuts, which sat in a bowl on the dining-room table, before eating a bite of the cheese. The parlor door creaked open. She wondered who had arrived, but exhaustion and hunger prevented her from putting on her socks and shoes once again. Her brother and his wife could meet the guest. Muffled conversations from the parlor drifted into the dining room.

Erina continued to eat before she pushed the plate away and rested her head on the table. She did not mean to fall asleep, but her eyes closed despite her best efforts. It had been a long night, and her sobs over the loss of her dear mother did not help.

"Erina," a voice cried.

She shook. Her eyelids shot open. She was about to rise to her feet when a male sat in the seat beside her.

Erina glanced at the handsome man. His bright blue eyes looked into hers. She recognized him but could not remember who he was. Something about that grin tugged at her brain.

"You don't remember me, Miss Erina?" he asked.

She studied him closer. He had a square jaw, and his slate-black hair shimmered in the afternoon sunlight. *Slate. Slate. School. Yes.* "You're Adam."

He nodded. "I can't believe you didn't remember the person who met you at the school door." He gave her a polite laugh.

"I was scared that day. You made it better."

"Not better for me that day." The corners of his lips curved up into a small smile.

"No, I guess I didn't. I'm sorry I got you in trouble," she responded in a low voice. Erina examined her former classmate's countenance. He did not look angry. However, she sensed he still held some resentment, probably from the confrontations she'd had in the past. She wondered why he came today. He only met her mother a couple of times. Her gaze widened as she stared at the clerical white collar. She swallowed the lump in her throat. "You're—you're the minister here?"

He nodded. "Well, yes. I bet that's difficult for you to believe."

She could not lie to a man of the cloth. She gulped and clasped her hands together, not uttering another word until she took a deep breath and spoke. "I–I –"

* * *

"Don't worry; I understand. We clashed a lot, but today we'll make amends, so we can honor your mother." He took her warm hand and held it for several seconds. His heart pounded in his chest. When Adam heard the news of Erina's mother's death, he knew this would make for a difficult day.

On one hand, Erina had an aura about her that drew him to her, but on the other hand, they were complete opposites. He liked nature, to fish and the farming life he grew up in and continued to do today, since the church had so few members. She favored the city life. He knew that was why she left Tekamah for the bigger city of Blair.

Adam stroked her hand a second to offer reassurance. "Would you like me to pray?"

"Yes." Tears flowed down Erina's cheeks. "I shouldn't have left. I should've stayed here and helped her with this …"

"With the farm?" added Adam. He ached for his former classmate. "You can't blame yourself. I'm sure she told you to seek your own journey."

"Uh-huh. But I knew I was leaving her all alone." She pulled her lace handkerchief from her skirt's pocket and wiped the droplets.

Adam's brow wrinkled. "But Erina, your brother is here, and you know this small community would help. We assist one another."

"The curse still wins out."

He wanted to ask what she was talking about. However, now while she grieved, he could not. Instead, he clamped his hand tighter around hers and whispered a prayer, "May the Lord wrap His loving arms around you. He knows what you're going through."

"I hope so," she murmured. Tears filled her eyes once more.

He shouldn't. He shouldn't. Everything told him not to; however, he did not know what else to do to comfort her, so he lightly pressed his warm lips on her forehead. He barely could stop. Taking a long breath, he wheezed out the words, "God will see you through."

"Or, will the curse win like it did before? Erina cried.

"He'll see you through, Erina, no matter what." Adam squeezed her hand tighter before he released his from hers.

Chapter Three

Erina stepped off her brother's buckboard and followed him and several of their male neighbors who carried the casket. Tears streaked down her face. She stumbled. A warm hand reached out to her. She grabbed it. "I'm sorry. I – I can't see."

"It's all right, Erina. I'll guide you."

She recognized that voice. "Thank you, Reverend Miller."

He gave a soft laugh. "Erina, you've known me since childhood. Please call me Adam."

"You sure?"

"Yes, and swear to me the only time you'll use the words reverend and Miller together is when you're at church."

"I do swear." His strong grip was comforting she had to admit.

Adam slowed his steps to keep pace with her.

The tall grasses swished against her ankles. This day overwhelmed her. After her father died ten years ago, she depended upon her mother to share Erina's joys, troubles and her everyday stresses. Her head ached, probably from all the crying.

Her mind went to the lovely mother of her youth. Ma was so pretty when she let her hair down. Her mother's soft brown hair flowed behind her ears and rested on her shoulders. Erina remembered her mother wearing a baby-blue long-sleeved jacket with front closure fitted over a matching ruffled skirt. In her gloved hand, she twirled the baby-blue parasol. Ma's lips spread into a sweet smile. Her mother was gleeful that day. Then tragedy struck. The smile vanished. Instead, they hastily left to travel here.

Erina heaved a heavy sigh. The hot spring sun beat down on her as she proceeded toward the gravesite. She wished to remove her hat to get more air floating around her face, but it would be unladylike to do such a thing.

Erina glanced at the tall headstone in front of her with its fancy writing, saying "In memory of Mr. Linus, son of Captain Oliver Linus." At least, he had a decent tombstone. Ma's would be a simple wooden cross buried next to her husband, Hershel Higgins. She struggled to take a breath while she maneuvered around it. Her skirt caught on the bottom edge of the stone. She stumbled and fell.

A strong arm lifted her up. "Here, take my hand."

"But I'm alright," she lied, knowing she should tell him the truth but was embarrassed to do so.

Adam gave a low chuckle. "Listen to me, Miss Erina Higgins, you've had a trying day, thus let the Lord and me carry you through."

Her hand shook. She wanted to reject his help; however, her weakened state would not allow her that privilege. Instead, she welcomed his firm and steady grip. She leaned her head on his comforting shoulder for a second before she pulled her head from his.

Adam wound around the headstones before they stopped several feet from the open grave, where the dug dirt lay. Erina screamed. Sobs ran down her cheeks. She jerked her hand from Adam's and raced toward the open grave. Adam caught up with her and braced her body to his. "Calm down, Erina. Calm down. Your ma is in Heaven."

"I know," she cried. "I want to join her. I can't live without her!"

"Yes, you can," he muttered into her ear. "It's not your time, sweetheart," he whispered. He separated from her and beckoned to Erina's brother to come over.

* * *

Sweetheart? Why, we're not courting. I don't even know you that well. Erina observed Adam while he stepped away from her and the family. With her dainty handkerchief, she wiped her wet teardrops. Adam glanced over at her. She released a long breath and nodded, signaling to him she was composed enough for him to begin her Ma's funeral.

His gaze scanned the group of neighbors and family members gathered around the gravesite. "The deceased was sixty-three years on this day. She was snatched away and missed the pleasure of seeing her grandchildren. Her husband passed ten years earlier, and now she will join her husband in richness."

What does he mean by "in richness"? Her ma had nothing. But this broken-down house and the Sunday dress she wore.

The preacher continued, "She loved her husband, and her children were her salt of the earth below our feet."

How do you know that? You were rarely over here. Then it dawned on Erina that perhaps he had visited and consoled her mother while Erina was away.

Adam's gaze settled on Erina's. He gulped. "Now she faces the cold, silent tomb to await the resurrection morn, when all the redeemed shall come forth glorified, bearing palms of victory." Adam lowered his body and reached down to pick up a handful of the rich, brown soil then straightened up to sprinkle the dirt onto the ground. "Ashes to ashes. Dust to Dust."

Erina screamed. Her brother hugged her and placed his palm over her mouth. Erina could feel the mourners' eyes upon her. She took a deep breath to get control of herself before sneaking a peek at her classmate. His steady gaze eased her qualms. She released a long breath.

"Let's pray," the minister proceeded. "Christ died for us, and His love will fill us with His peace as we go from here to continue our earthly lives. Amen."

* * *

I hope God fills me with His peace because I don't know how to go on without it. Erina stood next to her brother and her sister-in-law. She could not move. Her brother turned to her.

"Mary will stay here with you. I need to help lower the coffin and fill the grave."

"I know," Erna replied, lips trembling.

Lee maneuvered from his sister and moved forward. His wife advanced closer to Erina.

Her sister-in-law reached for Erina's hand and held it tight. "You all right?" Mary whispered.

"I think so," Erina muttered. Her fingers shook.

"There's a bench underneath that tree." Her brother's wife pointed to it. "We can sit and watch from there."

Erina hesitated but knew in her heart she needed to sit down in her weakened state. She nodded then followed her sister-in-law. They settled themselves on the narrow seat. Erina gazed at the men shoveling the dirt upon the grave. Tears dripped down her cheeks. She moaned.

Mary tightened her grip on her sister-in-law's hand. "Your ma was a sweet person. We'll miss her."

"Yes. Erina gulped then with her other hand, she dabbed the teardrops with her cloth.

"Do you smell the lovely apple blossoms?"

"I do. It's nice." Erina wiggled on the hard seat. The dirt continued to pile upon the grave. She struggled not to scream again. Soon the agony would go away, but the ache would never leave her.

Mary cleared her throat and released her hand from Erina's. "I didn't know you knew the preacher."

"Uh-huh. We were in school together. He's older than me."

"Did you meet him before you started school?"

"No, we hadn't been here that long." *Mary sure was inquisitive. She was conjuring up a courtship between Erina and Adam. She likes to partner people up and now I'm probably her next victim. Oh why, did I have to run into him? I never really liked him. We are such opposites. I know opposites attract but we're like winter and summer. I'm cold-hearted, except for my family, and he's outwardly reserved but caring.*

"It looks like they're about finished," Mary explained. Would you like us to spend the night with you?"

She would love that, but her saddened condition could cause crying outbursts, and she would not want to expose these to them. "No, I'd rather grieve by myself tonight." She gulped. "However, if Lee would assist me with the morning chores for the next few days, I would appreciate it."

"Agreed."

She and Mary were not close, but she was a caring person, and Erina was happy she wanted to help her.

Chapter Four

Erina blew out the kerosene light on the nightstand. She dropped her body onto her mother's bed with a thump. The coil springs squeaked. Not caring, she snuggled between the sheets and her mother's square-in-a-square quilt. She remembered her ma's struggle to make the quilt since she had never done an undertaking like that before. In their old life, they had the luxury of purchasing quilts that others had made. She smiled, remembering that time of happiness.

Then the tears fell softly down her cheeks. She rubbed them off with her fists. Erina could not see how she could sleep tonight. But grief and weariness caused her to fall into a sound slumber.

Erina opened her eyelids wide to the crow of a rooster. She shook her head to awaken from her sleep. Scanning the bedroom, she stared at the strange room with the light glow of the morning sunlight lighting the room. Her gaze went to the dresser, which held the water bowl and matching pitcher. Then she glanced at the wooden rocker with her olive-green dress draped over the chair's back.

It was then Erina realized she lay in her mother's bed, and she would continue to do so until school restarted in the fall. Could she handle it? She did not know, but somehow she would muster the strength. Erina stretched out her arms and yawned. The cluck, cluck of the chickens awoke her to the conclusion that her brother must be out there.

Throwing off the quilt, she jumped up. She in quick speed made the bed, picked up the pitcher then poured the liquid into the bowl. Erina then grabbed the cloth that sat beside it before dabbing her face and underarms. Reaching for her long-sleeved, cotton frock, she slipped it over her head. This was one of her teacher dresses. The other one hung inside the wardrobe.

Slipping into her black leather boots with their square heels, she laced them and rushed out the front door. "Lee! Lee! Are you out here?" she shouted.

To the cluck of the hens, Erina entered the chicken coop. One chicken flew down, rocked back and forth then flapped her tail wings. Erina edged toward the door, for she did not want more hens to follow that one's lead.

Maybe he's in the barn to milk Daisy. As she maneuvered up the small hill toward it, Erina again called out for her brother. No response. She took another step and yelled, "Lee! Lee!" No answer. A twig snapped behind her. She jumped.

A voice laughed.

Erina turned around. Her brow furrowed while she looked straight into the reverend's gaze. "What – what are you doing here?"

Adam chuckled. "I came to help you. Remember I'm a farmer and a minister."

Her cheeks warmed. "Oh, why, thank you, but my brother is to come so I don't –

"Need my assistance," he interrupted. "But you do, for I sent Lee home and told him I would take care of the chores today."

Her mouth opened wide before she shut it. "Well, there's no need. Really I'd hate to impose upon you." Adam was becoming a nuisance. She admired his help, but she also needed some time to grieve and did not want him around.

Erina's mind returned to a schoolyard incident, which was one of several past encounters with him.

The girls were taking turns jumping rope, and the boys were playing baseball. Erina could hear the boys shouting in the schoolyard field, "Run! Run! John."

However, Erina had not wanted to jump rope that day, so she had slipped away from the girls and strode to the swings. She had settled onto the hard wooden seat and had pumped to lift herself up high in the air before she had regulated the speed to a more moderate tempo.

The crisp autumn air had brushed against her shoulders. In the distance, she had seen the tree limbs sway in the breeze. She remembered closing her eyes a minute to enjoy the splendor of seeing golden and rust leaves sprouting the trees. It was then someone had pushed her swing. Her hands had lost their grip on the ropes, and she had fallen to the ground.

A boy's laughter had echoed around her. She had glanced up to see Adam, who stood in front of her.

His large smile turned to concern. "You're not hurt. I – I didn't mean to do that. I wanted to –"

"You're a naughty boy," Erina intervened. "I should tell Miss Clarke."

"Please don't! I just wanted to have some fun." Adam reached out his arm.

She grasped it then he pulled her up. She dusted the dirt off her long skirt. "Adam,

you're nothing but trouble. Besides, you shouldn't be here with the girls. That alone should have gotten you a whipping."

He gave her a sorrowful look before rushing back to the boys.

Why had she not tattled on him? He did not deserve her sympathies.

"Erina! Erina!" Her name reverberated in her ears, bringing her back to the present. She looked up at Adam.

"Are you alright? I've been shouting your name while you were in a daze."

"I'm fine. Thanks for your help. I'll take care of the eggs if you want to do the rest."

He nodded then smiled.

Erina had to find a way to make him leave. Her mind scrambled to think of excuses. She gazed downward and swayed back and forth. When she glanced up to meet Adam's gaze, she was stunned to view an empty space. The minister must have left to do the rest of the chores without her knowing. *He's so aggravating. I wish he would stay away. I can't stand him!* She gulped knowing that type of thinking was not Christian.

* * *

Adam creaked open the dilapidated barn door then hastened inside. The black-and-white spotted Holstein cow met him near the entrance. She mooed. "Did I startle you?" Adam made his voice calm as he talked to the cow. "Now you're going to be fine. We just need a little milk."

The reverend scanned the barn to search for the milking stool and a metal pail. He spotted them in a southwest corner and strode to them. Pulling out the rag inside the metal pail, he cleaned the udder. The cow mooed again. *She senses I'm a stranger.*

"Calm down, Daisy. You stand still and this will go quickly." Grasping the udder, he began squeezing the milk. Daisy shifted her hoofs one time, but soon the job was finished. "You're a good girl. I'll bring in some hay for you to eat later." The cow mooed once more. "I know you want it now, but you've still got some, and I promise I'll make sure I'll bring you some before I leave." He smiled.

Carrying the bucket of milk with one hand, Adam opened the door. He had wanted to do the chores to help make up for his school-days misdeeds. He was a troublemaker in his youth. After he found Christ, he changed, and he hoped Erina would see that.

He angled his feet down the small hill while balancing the milk. He passed the chicken coop and reached the front door. He knocked lightly. Then he waited a minute for Erina before he proceeded inside.

Wiping her hand on her long white apron, she approached him. "I'm sorry I was in the kitchen. Put the milk in there."

He nodded and followed her into the room. "Where should I set it?"

"Place it on the worktable, and I'll get a pitcher where we can pour the milk into it." Erina stepped toward the cabinet then grabbed the china pitcher decorated with lavender and white flowers.

He cleared his throat. "Shouldn't we put the milk in the icebox?"

"No, because we'll need it for our coffee."

"Coffee?"

"Yes, I made some. You do like fried eggs and toast, don't you?"

"Why, yes." She puzzled him. Why did she invite him to stay? Had her heart softened toward him, or was it to repay him for doing the chores? He gazed at her.

"You're making me nervous, Erina replied. She placed the iron skillet on the

stove then grabbed the lard before she spooned some into the pan. "How many eggs do you want and how do you like them?"

"I'll take three since I haven't had fried eggs in a long time and over easy. What can I do to help?" Adam looked forward to such a nice breakfast. He usually had toast and then spurted out the door to do the chores and visit congregants.

"No help needed. I have everything under control. Why not take a seat at the table?" She inserted the bread into a wire contraption with long handles before she returned to crack the eggs into the hot grease, three for him and two for her.

Adam made his way to the table and settled onto a seat. Hunger pains arose. He inhaled the odor of the frying eggs and toast cooking. Without meaning to, his gaze settled on her behind. *What a shapely rear and nice hips.* His heart raced. He took a deep breath to calm himself. She flipped over the eggs before she placed them on the gold-edged plates with violet flowers. The second round of toast turned brown on one side, so she turned it over. He wanted to run to her and give her a long kiss. *Relax. relax,* he told his heart.

Gripping a potholder, she released the toast and placed it on the plates. She strode to him, opened the cabinet's drawer then reached for the silverware. Erina smiled. Spotting the jam sitting on the open shelf, she turned to him. "Do you like homemade strawberry jam?"

"Oh, am I a lucky man today. Well yes, I would love some."

"Ma made it." She stepped to him and presented him his gold-edged with purple and white flowered plate. Then she reached for the preserves. "The jam is so good. We had a good crop of strawberries last year, and she decided to learn how to make these." Her hands shook. She took a deep breath before she set it on the table. She wobbled.

Adam jumped up to steady her. He wrapped his arms tight around her. His mouth nuzzled against the faint scent of soap in her hair. His heart thundered inside his chest. He took a deep breath and maneuvered his mouth from her hair. "You've got to take it easy. Rest is what you need."

"I'm fine now. I just miss her so much." Erina strode to the coffee pot and poured the hot liquid into two cups before she returned with them.

"Let me get the milk and your plate."

"You sure?" Erina asked in a meek voice.

"Yes."

"But your eggs will get cold," she pleaded.

"I'm not worried. I've eaten eggs that sat a lot longer than this. When a man is hungry, he doesn't care." Adam laughed, picked up the cups before he brought them to the table. He returned with Erina's plate and the milk. "Now who uses cream?"

"I don't." She giggled.

"I don't either. So we saved this milk for coffee, and yet we both like our coffees black." He chuckled, realizing for the first time they had no hostility between them.

Chapter Five

Erina sipped her coffee. Her tears had subsided. She glanced at her handsome former schoolmate with his slate-black hair combed back from his brow. She knew she was attracted to him, but yet her heart would not allow her to forgive him for his past deeds. She had made him breakfast, for she was grateful for him coming today.

She gazed up at him, taking in his bright blue eyes, which now had a special glow to them. Erina swallowed the hot liquid before cutting into her egg and chewing the egg white.

"This breakfast is such a treat for me," chimed in Adam after he took a bite of his toast. "I'm grateful you invited me to stay, and this strawberry jam your ma made is wonderful."

"She was so excited to learn how to do this." His comments about her mother almost brought her to tears, but she forced them back. Erina steadied her hand to prevent it from trembling before she grabbed her coffee cup. "I helped Ma last year with making the jelly."

"Doing the jam was work and was so much fun," Erina continued. "I could tell Ma's health was failing, but Ma had willpower and had determination. We laughed at putting too much jam in some of the jars until we learned not to fill them too full. Then we placed the rubber rings and clamped the lids on the containers." Erina swallowed some of the coffee. "Ma always was a fighter even after we left New York and came here …"

"Why did you leave New York? I always wondered about that." Adam examined Erina's countenance.

"I don't want to speak about it." Her hands shook. She jerked them under the table and clasped her fingers together to quell the shaking. Erina shifted her gaze from Adam before she reengaged him. "We'll talk about more pleasant things this morning." Her family's secret was too heartbreaking to reveal. Taking a deep breath, she returned her hands to the table to finish her breakfast. "Again, I thank you for coming today, and I am sure Lee was relieved."

"Yes, he was. He has quite a spread of his own." Adam smiled. "He needs to start having a bunch of children. That would help him."

Erina laughed. "It sure would, wouldn't it? It's difficult to believe my little brother is married. He always will be my little Lee."

"He sure doesn't look like a *little Lee* to me."

"I know with him being almost six feet tall and having those muscular biceps, he is more like one of those big-city boxers."

"You're right about that one," he replied in a light and airy tone.

Erina took the last bite of her toast. She hated the breakfast to end. It was nice to have company after such a difficult time. She stood up, and Adam presented her his plate before he picked up the milk.

"I could come tomorrow if you wish." His gaze met hers.

She shook her head, knowing she still was skeptical about the childhood troublemaker becoming a reverend.

"Oh no, I don't want to impose. My brother can do the honors."

"You sure?" Adam peered at her, taking in her facial features.

Heat rose to her cheeks. She would love to have him here each morning. However, she knew she still did not trust the supposedly changed man before her. "It is almost planting time, and you'll need to do that. Lee can do the planting, and, in fact, he'll love that since, with this farm and his own, we'll have more produce."

"That's fine. I'll stop by and see how you're doing."

The jolt in her stomach surprised her. Did he mean he actually cared about her?

* * *

Disappointed at not being able to see Erina for some time, Adam headed down the small hill and angled toward his place. Actually, it was not his; it was his parents'. However, he did most of the work since both Pa and Ma were not as agile as they had been in their earlier days. He was the youngest of seven children. All the others had left home and had spread out across Nebraska – and one even to Iowa. Some were farmers or farmer wives, and one became a Lincoln attorney through an apprentice program.

He missed his sprawling family and how many hands made the work light. However, with his siblings gone, days were full from dawn to dark in conjunction with his ministerial duties. He picked his way through the growing weeds as he descended the hill. The warm sun beat on his forehead. He wondered when he would see Erina next.

Between it all, I have to see her or I'll lose her. She would return to her school duties in the fall, and he wanted her as his own before she left. How would he do this? He did not know. However, he needed to come up with something.

Looking over the horizon, his parents' place came into view. The pump stood several feet near the five porch posts spamming the front façade. The wooden planks needed painting, but that would wait for now. That gave Adam an idea. *Hmm. Yes, Erina's place needs painting.* Adam smiled. *Yes, this would give me an excuse to see her.* He would paint her house. The paint would give it a fresh look. His lips curved up into a smile as he reached his parents' home. He had his answer. Now he needed to implement his plan.

* * *

Two weeks later, Erina stepped toward the chicken coop. Clucks, clucks, clucks met her ears while she stepped around the red-combed hens while she spread the chicken feed on the ground. She giggled. "Alright, welcoming committee. I got your message. I know I'm not the usual egg gatherer."

The high-and-mighty rooster strutted around the coop with his midnight-black feathered tail arched high. He stood like a soldier waiting for battle. Erina maneuvered around him. He could be mean at times, and she did not want to get kicked by the rooster's spurs. She picked up her pace, swung open the slanted, wooden coop's door and entered.

The foul odor reached her nostrils. She had been so distraught she had let her brother take care of all the chores, and yet she knew, in her heart, he was rushing these so he could return to do his own chores. *I guess I really can't blame him. That should be his focus.* She reached up to grab a saddle-brown egg from the hen's nest. One after another she gathered the eggs until she had several. *This will make for a good breakfast.*

Thinking of breakfast made her think of Adam. They did have a nice time two weeks earlier. She still did not understand why she invited him to breakfast that day. Of course, she wanted to thank him. However, it was more than that. She shook her head. *No, I can't be attracted to a man who caused me so much trouble. I'm not. I'm not drawn to him!* Adjusting the egg basket in her arms, she headed for the house.

She must not fall in love with him, or any man for that matter. Once they learned of her family's secret, it all would be over. A teardrop trickled down her cheek. It would take a certain man to overcome her secret. Even a man of the cloth may have trouble forgiving. *Oh Lord, what am I to do?* She clamped her lips together while her mind returned to the days before they left New York.

Her mother stood in the large formal parlor where ruby-red draped curtains tied back with gold tassels exposed the two long, wide windows. Erina shivered. She looked up at her lovely mother, dressed in a tan long dress decorated with a white-laced collar and a laced trimmed hem. Her ma's usual smiling eyes were smothered in tears. In her hand, Ma held a linen handkerchief. She sobbed and wiped away the fallen teardrops.

"Ma, what's wrong?" Erina's quivering lips asked.

"It's awful." She stepped to the piano and glanced out one of the windows. "I've loved this house but – but we've got to leave."

"Leave?"

"Yes, sweetheart. You know about sin and how God does not like that?"

I nodded.

"Well, today the secret was revealed, and Ma and Pa must leave and never come back."

"Never?" Erina's lips trembled.

"That's right. Never."

"Ma, what's the secret? Wouldn't God forgive? I don't understand."

"I'll tell you the full story when you get older. Right now, you're too young to understand," Ma's voice almost was a whisper. Mother revealed the whole truth years later.

I wished she hadn't because that secret should've stayed hidden, Erina thought. *Now I'm saddled with it and must protect my family's reputation.* Only she knew the hidden truth.

Chapter Six

The rooster crowed. Erina's eyes popped open. She yawned and stretched her arms out. Through her ma's lace curtains, the sunrays streaked across her mother's square-in-a-square quilt. Since her mother's death in early April, Erina had not gone to church, knowing at any moment she might burst into tears. Today, though, Erina's stolen energy returned to her, and she decided it was time to return.

Not going to church on the Sabbath gnawed at her. She must seek God's face and ask for His forgiveness for her non-attendance. She clamped her lips together to keep them from quivering. Erina took a deep breath. It was time to see old faces and praise the Almighty for comforting her during her mourning.

Pushing off the quilt, Erina stood in front of the water basin and poured the cool liquid into the bowl. Grabbing the small towel, she wet it before she picked it up and rubbed the homemade soap onto the cloth. The droplets washed over her from the neck, underarms and her upper body.

What should I wear? Her mind raced through the items in her mother's wardrobe from the tan linen shirtwaist trimmed with a lace collar and around the sleeves to a royal blue checkered dress with flouncy sleeves to the ivory lightweight cotton dress decorated with an eyelet bodice and hem. Erina smiled. *Yes, yes, the eyelet shirtwaist is perfect with its flowing skirt.*

She stepped to the wide window and cracked open the sash to let the late April fresh air float inside. *All right God, I hear you calling. I'm going. I'm going.* She headed for the wardrobe, unlocked the door and lifted the ivory dress off the rod. Holding the light fabric in her hand, she held it close to her chest then danced around the room until she became dizzy and sat on the bed. *Oh Lord, thanks for making me feel alive again.* Tears of joy fell down her cheeks. The days of mourning were beginning to vanish.

She stood in her petticoat then slipped on the ivory dress. She stepped to the nightstand to grab the large-brim straw hat decorated with a wide ivory bow on the middle. She gazed at her image in the wardrobe's small mirror. The hat swooped leftward, and the brim rested over her left eyebrow. Erina grinned at the effect while she put on her ivory gloves. Then she grabbed her parasol, opened the door and headed down the hill.

The trip down the hill reminded her of her childhood school days. She inhaled the fresh dewdrops, which dotted the weed blades and tickled her ankles as she maneuvered around them. A spattering of ruby-red wildflowers graced the edge of the slope. She drank in the spring air, rejoicing for the first time in its loveliness. Erina reached the schoolhouse then turned right to head for Cross Lutheran Church. It was quite a walk but a nice trek during springtime.

Erina's heart jumped with joy as she viewed the small white structure with its cross steeple and arched windows on each side of the entrance door. She swung the door open and entered. Standing inside the doorway was Adam with his hand stretched outward and his bright blue eyes staring into hers. She gulped. *Well, you got me here, God. Now what?*

* * *

Hand trembling, Adam shook Erina's warm hand. Her presence made his heart race. He wanted so to kiss those luscious lips, but instead he took a deep breath. He must calm his nerves, for after all, he had to preach and have clean thoughts. The reverend greeted businessman Lucas Pierce and his wife and their young boys, ages four to ten, all wearing wool chocolate-brown suits. He shook each of their hands and especially enjoyed shaking the little hand of the youngest whose fingertips barely reached the minister's palm.

With a snobbish look, Mrs. Nielsen rushed inside. Shoulders arched, chin tilted upright, she gave a half smile. "Running a little late today." She panted. "Hope you're going to center your message on some of the loose morals around here."

Adam gulped and put on a smile. He knew she was talking about her neighbors who allowed their teenage daughter to spend time with a thirty-year-old man. It was disgraceful. He shook her hand. "I'm sorry but today's sermon is an uplifting one. Spring is here, thus my topic will focus on God's creation."

"Well, they created that daughter of theirs and allowed that immoral behavior." Mrs. Nielsen took a step forward. "It's time they reaped the consequences of their actions."

"Perhaps, but it's in God's hands."

"Ugh!" Mrs. Nielsen replied. Then she marched to the front pew where she always sat.

Pulling out his pocket watch, Adam glanced at the time and made his way toward the front. He looked over at the love of his life, Erina, who sat in the third-row pew. He took a deep breath and steadied his steps toward the pulpit.

The young and pretty blonde-headed organist, Miss Pepperdine, placed her hands on the pipe organ's keys and ground out the hymn, *Love Divine, all Love excelling, Joy of heav'n, to earth come down, Fix in us Thy humble dwelling, all Thy faithful mercies crown, Jesus, Thou art all compassion, Pure, unbounded love Thou art; Visit us with Thy salvation, Enter ev – 'ry trembling heart . . .*

** * **

Erina listened to the opening tune and sighed. *Such a beautiful hymn.* She smiled, glancing up at her old childhood schoolmate. He stepped to the pulpit with assurance. Adam had a leadership quality about him. She never saw that in him during their school days, but the Lord must have brought out the best in him. He gazed at her and Erina's heart raced. She gulped. Never had a man done that to her before, and this frightened her, for she could not have these feelings with her past hovering around her.

She stiffened her shoulders and listened to Adam's opening remarks.

He scanned the room and grinned. "I see several new people in attendance, and I want to welcome you to Cross Lutheran. You will find us to be a friendly lot. Please join us outside for a glass of punch and cookies after service." His gaze settled on Erina.

She cringed. *I can't stay. I've got to go home.* Erina clasped her shaking hands together. How would she avoid him with those refreshments served on the front lawn? Erina bit her lower lip while Adam continued the worship. At last, the church service ended. Her only hope was to rush to the exit before people congregated around the punch bowl.

The ushers stood at the first row to release those sitting there. Then they came to the second row. Congregants stood up and headed toward the exit. The men, wearing suits, nodded before she and the other four parishioners in her row got to their feet and marched toward the doorway. Erina scooted around one group of talkative adults in front of her. Releasing a long breath, she hastened her steps to get to the door. Her heart rate quickened. The exit was in her grasp!

"Erina, Erina! It's so good to see you."

She shifted her gaze to the voice and stood still until the heavy-set woman rushed to her.

"Why, I haven't seen you in ages." Her old classmate reached out her hand to Erina.

Erina grasped her friend's thick fingers. "It's good to see you." They stood there for a minute then the woman behind them bumped into them. Erina opened her mouth to speak.

"Wait for me outside. We'll talk then," the plump lady stated.

Trapped, Erina strode outside to wait. Men were setting up tables while several women readied the host table of punch, glasses and two trays of cookies. Her stomach roiled. *I want to go home. I can't stay.* She glimpsed around her, wanting to make sure she avoided Adam. He had not yet appeared. She released a long breath. A breeze floated around her. It lifted the hem of her skirt, exposing her ankles. Her cheeks warmed. Erina pushed her skirt down and shifted her feet. *Where is Bertha?*

With each minute, more people gathered outside. *I've got to get home before Adam comes outside. Come on, Bertha!*

"Who you searching for?" a male voice said in a laughing tone.

Erina rotated around to face the familiar voice. Her cheeks became hot. "I—I am waiting for a classmate."

"You mean like me?" Adam teased.

"Well, no!" Her lips quivered. "She's a girl."

"You mean like you?" His eyes sparkled.

"Uh, well, yes."

"Didn't you know God only made one of you?"

Erina tugged at the three-quarter-length sleeves. *Why did he get the better of her?* She shifted her balance from one foot to the other. *Where was that friend of her*s? Finally, the plump classmate arrived. "Well, I see the minister has cornered you. He always has favored you."

"I—I don't know about that. We sparred a lot."

Adam chuckled. "That's for sure. I'd better mingle with the rest of the congregation, so I'll leave you two to rekindle the old days." He stretched out his hand to Erina and Bertha before he made his way to the rest of the congregants outside.

Once out of sight, the overweight classmate began to talk. "You didn't recognize me at first, did you?"

"Well, yes and no. I recognized you, but I couldn't remember your name at first. It's been quite a while since we were in school."

Bertha laughed. "I know, and I've put on a little weight since our school days."

You have thought as she studied her friend. "You were such a skinny thing."

Bertha nodded. "I was, but now I'm a happy contented woman with two boys, a wealthy husband and a potbelly."

That would do it. Erina chuckled.

Bertha scanned the punch line. "My husband and family are gesturing to me to join them. I'd better go but we'll get together."

"Yes, we will. I look forward to it." Erina smiled while she studied the outside refreshment tables and how to maneuver around them without being seen.

Chapter Seven

Erina stepped around the fern plant to pull the parlor's laced curtains apart. She shook her head now happy she could open the large window, bringing in soft spring breezes.

Today marked the first day Erina had a resignation of peace about her mother's death. Thank the good Lord for allowing her the time to begin healing before she returned to teaching in September.

She took a deep breath. *Is that what I want?* She no longer knew what she wanted. Staying with this family or that family throughout the school year sure did not lead to her having her own house or someone who loved her. *Oh, stop daydreaming, Erina.* She shook her head. Oh, how could she think that way when the family's secret would scare any man away?

A knock on the door erased her thoughts. She made her way to the door. In one way, she hoped it was her minister friend, and in another way, she hoped not. *I cannot break his heart, and if I continue, I will.* Erina opened the door. She forced herself to smile at her brother. "Well, it's good to see you."

"I know I haven't been over here like I planned, but I gathered the eggs and fed the animals."

"Thank you. I'm glad you did those this morning."

Lee smiled. "I see you've done a great job in doing those chores, but when the produce starts coming in, I'll make sure I'm here every day."

"Why, that's nice of you, Lee."

"Well, you know I love my sister."

She swallowed the lump in her throat. *Yes, but at times, you're more concerned about what your wife wants.* "Come on inside, and we'll talk a bit." Erina swung the door open.

Lee entered. "Mary went to see her folks, so I thought I'd come here.

"Glad you did." *At least now I know why you stopped by.* Erina led him to the dining room. "I'll put on the teapot, and we'll sip tea like Ma and Pa did back East."

Lee settled in a dining-room chair. "You'll have to tell me more about their big house. I was too little to remember."

"Yes, I'll do that, as much as I can remember; after all, I was only seven years old when we left New York."

Erina pumped water into the kettle and placed it on the stove to heat. After it heated, she placed the loose tealeaves into the pot and poured the hot liquid over it. She returned to the dining room and took a seat beside her brother. "Tea will be done after it steeps."

"Sounds good. I look forward to a cup."

"I know." A tear dripped down her cheek. She wiped it with her fingertip. "Ma's death still hurts."

"It does," chimed in Lee. "She was a good Ma. I loved the way she could add this and that to a dish she was making and make it last for days."

"She had that knack. It especially was something since she had servants until she came here. We had a jolly Negro woman who knew how to make delicious meals and also made wonderful baked goods." Erina scrunched her nose. "I still can remember the sweet taste of the Knobby apple she used along with a more bitter variety from Rhode Island to make those delicious apple muffins."

"How do you know this?" chimed in Lee. His lips curled into a small smile.

"Well, I watched her make them and she told me. I always bothered her in the kitchen." Erina chuckled. "I licked the spoon, and the maid would point her finger and say, 'Child, you quit or tell yo Ma.' I would look up at her and say in a soft-toned voice, 'You wouldn't do that, would you, Mama?' She would rush over, put her large arms around me and hug me tight. 'No, child, I ain't goin' to do that, but yo stop licking that spoon or I'll …'"

'Or what?' I said teasing. For I knew she loved me and enjoyed having me in the kitchen." Erina paused before she returned to face her brother. "The last thing I did," her lips trembled, "was to pour the batter in the tins."

"Why? I want to know the reason. Tell me the secret," urged Lee.

"I wish I could," Erina muttered, "but some things are better not told." Erina stood up and stepped into the kitchen to retrieve the teapot and cups. She placed the pink rose teapot, accented with a gold spout and handle and its matching saucers and cups, on the tray.

Setting the tray on the dining-room table, she presented the saucers and teacups in front of Lee then poured the hot tea into his cup before she did her own. "Tea helps relax you, and after Ma's death, we need a little of that." Erina smiled then settled into her seat.

* * *

Lee sipped the hot liquid. "Tastes good. I remember Ma serving tea. It must be an Irish custom."

"Oh, it's more than that. It brings cheer, calms fears and keeps the Irish warm during rainy days." Erina took a drink then returned the cup to the saucer.

Lee took another sip of the soothing tea before he renewed his conversation about his parents' past. "I can understand how the secret was not shared with me. I was too young. However, I'm a man now and want to know what happened." He stared at the cup's contents, waiting several moments for his sister to respond.

"I don't want to share it. It's devastating." Her lips quivered.

"I can handle it, sis. I need to know." He gulped. "I must know," he muttered.

Erina fiddled with her left curl. Her body shook. She took a deep breath. "I will," she muttered, adding, "but now is the wrong time." She gasped. "Did you hear that?"

"What?" he asked in exasperation.

"That sound?" she replied as she stood up and rushed to the dining-room windows to pull the golden-yellow Chintz cotton curtains further apart. Eyes wide, she leaned her head on the glass. "Someone is out there!" She cupped her hands and placed them on her hips. "Really, Lee, I'm not hearing things."

His brow furrowed. He opened his mouth to speak.

She stared at her brother with fear in her eyes. "See, I told you!"

He was about to throw up his hands in disgust when the clanging sound reached his ears. "I heard it!" he shouted. "Don't move!"

Erina nodded, her face white as snow-capped mountains.

"Don't worry. I'll take care of it!" He pushed the front door open and rushed outside.

* * *

Erina's body shook. The clanging spooked her. *What if Lee hadn't been here?* Erina shook her head. *Why am I trembling?* In a small community, she should not worry about safety, but yet here she was, frightened. Taking a deep breath, she assessed her behavior. *Of course, it's Ma's death.* Ever since her mother's departure, she had worried her mother's sin would lead to her own. It was inconceivable, but yet the Lord could hold her responsible for not exposing the sin.

And yet, if she exposed the truth, the secret could destroy her family's reputation. She could not divulge it. Erina had to stay quiet. She paced the dining-room floor. What did Lee find? She pressed her hands on her dress's gathered skirt. She gulped.

The more she fretted, the more intense she became. She took a deep breath to calm herself. However, her racing heart would not pause. She continued to pace the floor. Her low midnight-black heels clicked across the floorboards.

Erina took a long breath. Her heart rate accelerated. *Keep calm. Keep calm,* she told herself. She took another deep breath. But her anxiety overwhelmed her, and she raced out the door. *I've got to know.*

Her brother, who stood by an elm tree, waved her over. The other person's back faced her. She ran pell-mell into her brother's arms.

* * *

"All right, sis," Lee said in a laughing tone.

"But, but ..." Her arms shivered.

"Calm down," her brother added.

"Not with that man's back facing me," she whispered.

Lee raised his voice to the unidentified person. "Turn around! My sister wants to know who you are."

The man slowly turned to Erina.

Her mouth opened wide. "What are you doing here, Adam?"

"I stopped by so you could make me breakfast."

She laughed. "It's a little late for that since breakfast was served hours ago." She looked him in the eye. "What's the real reason you're here?"

"I – I came here to paint your house."

"Paint my house? I don't believe that. What's the real reason you're here?"

"To paint your house," Adam answered with a chuckle in his voice.

Exasperated, Erina placed her hands on her hips. She turned to her brother. "What's he really up to?"

"To paint our mother's house," her brother answered.

"Prove it to me. I don't believe either one of you." Her gaze went from her brother to Adam. "I demand the truth!"

"You do?" chimed in Adam. "We're telling you the truth." His lips spread into a quirky smile.

Adam always had a way of raising her temper like the school day he snuck up behind her to push her off the swing. Erina stroked her chin. *What are the two of you up to?*

Adam stood stoic before his lips parted and a chuckle escaped. "I'm here to help, and painting is what I'm here to do along with the expectation of a tasty dinner."

"Tasty dinner. Why, you can expect that until the cows come home. I'm— I'm not doing that," she stammered in exasperation.

"Of course, you will. You wouldn't want to leave hungry men without sustenance?" the minister asked with a twinkle in his eye.

"Oh, yes I would. You two can fend for yourselves," she retorted before she placed her hands on her hips.

Lee stared at his sister then said with exasperation, "Make some tea then and some of those leftover teacakes would be nice." He turned to Adam. "Start your painting!"

"You two are making me mad with your lies. Stop it! Right now!" she yelled, stomping her right foot in frustration.

"Maybe I lied to you in the past, Erina, but I'm a changed man now." Adam pulled out his large red kerchief from his back pocket, wiping his brow before he returned it to his pocket. He grabbed the pail in front of him then reached for the bucket underneath his feet. "Here's your proof!"

"That pail? That doesn't prove a thing!"

Her brother chimed in, "Look inside that bucket, and you'll find he's not lying to you! Now get out of his way, so he can get to it."

Could she really believe Adam was a changed man? She doubted it but stepped toward him. He presented her with the bucket. She looked inside and saw the white paint. "I'm sorry. I believe you."

He grabbed the pail from her.

She knew he was angry. *Could a leopard really change his spots?* She still questioned his ability to do so. Yet, he did study to become a minister and his manner was one of caring, which, of course, was the opposite of what he used to be. She lifted her head to her brother to ask him what he thought, but he was no longer there. *Where did he go?*

Chapter Eight

Lee stood in front of Adam at the elm tree. "What part of the house are you going to paint first?"

"I thought I'd start with the porch and go around the windows."

"Good idea." Lee looked over at the barn. "Inside that barn is a ladder."

"Thanks, but I won't need it right now. I can reach the window trim and porch railings, but when I get close to doing the porch's eaves, I'll need it."

"Alright. You had my sister frightened when she heard that bang."

"I didn't mean to scare her. A gust of wind slammed the metal pail into that tree, which distributed the paint equally. I wanted to clean things up around here. After all, your elderly mother was not able to do them."

"Yes." Lee gave him a sly smile. "But I think the real reason you are here is because you're sweet on my sister."

"Um. I—I—"

"I thought so. You've got your hands full with her. She doesn't much cotton to the way you treated her in school." Lee winked at the minister.

"I know. I was quite mischievous then. I've changed." Adam shifted his feet then grabbed the bucket. "I've got to get painting."

"What made you change?" Lee shouted as Adam strode toward the porch.

* * *

Adam examined the white peeled paint on the porch's posts. Although he had stopped in to visit Erina's ma when she was alive, he had paid little attention to the exterior of the house. *I'm happy I decided to do this.*

He pulled out his knife to scrape the peeled paint from the posts. He did this with quick motions so the paint in his pail did not harden before he applied it. Once done, he wiped the posts with a clean cloth then put on a coat of paint on each of the three porch posts. He smiled at the progress he was making. Engrossed in his work, he began to whistle as he moved the brush up and down.

The spring breeze prickled the back of his neck as he painted. He needed to get as much done as possible since he had ministerial duties to perform, and he had to take care of his family's farm. He thought of Erina being scared at the bang of his bucket against the tree. He chuckled.

"What are you laughing at?" a voice reverberated behind him.

He turned around to face Erina. His cheeks were warm while he studied her, the cute girl he had been infatuated with during his school days. The warm breeze whisked around them, picking up her fine locks and returning them to rest upon her brow. She pushed them to the side of her face.

She turned her gaze from him to examine the posts. The white paint sparkled in the sunlight. "You're doing a great job. I can't thank you enough." She paused. "I really did not see how they needed painting. Thank you."

"You're welcome." The corners of his lips spread into a smile. "You've had a lot on your mind so it's understandable you wouldn't notice."

"I appreciate that. After Pa died, I centered my existence on Ma. In my heart, I knew she was not well but she always persevered." Her voice broke. "I just – just couldn't contemplate her dying." She wiped the dripping teardrop with her fingertip. "Now there's no one."

Adam put his paintbrush into the pail and set the bucket on the wooden porch. He stepped to her and studied her sad countenance. "Don't blame yourself. You did the best you could." He forced his voice from breaking up. "When the Lord says it's your time, it's your time. She was failing. Barely could walk or take care of herself."

"I know, but it didn't help that I ran off to take this position, and Ma had no one to look after her."

Adam reached for Erina's hand and stroked her fingers. "Now you stop this. Your brother was here." Adam's spoke in weak tones. "I was here."

"Why were you? I'm baffled by that." Erina gazed up at Adam.

"Because I loved her like she was my second mother." He pressed his hand over Erina's.

"But you hardly knew her. At least, I had no knowledge of you seeing her."

He stroked her hand again. "You weren't here. I came to visit her, preached the Gospel and helped her around the house." He did as he told Erina, but he knew he visited Erina's ma more because she was the mother of the one he adored.

Erina gazed up at Adam, her eyes meeting his. She held the gaze a minute before speaking. "I'm happy you took care of her."

"Glad to do it." He took a deep breath.

"Ma believed in God but not a big believer in attending church. She made Lee and me go while she and Pa stayed home."

"You're not the only family that did that. Parents want their children to learn about Jesus. However, they themselves do not often attend." He paused. "I've never understood why they do that, but they do."

Erina looked down at the porch floor. "I think I know why Ma and Pa didn't go."

"Why?" he asked.

"Can't say."

"You can tell me. Preachers are sworn to keep things confidential." He smiled.

"I can't." Erina backed away from him.

"I promise I won't share it with anyone, except the Lord." Even when he was young, he knew something was amiss with her family. "You can tell me," he yelled as she spun around and rushed toward her brother.

* * *

Erina reached her brother, who stood underneath that elm tree with his back to her. *I'm surprised my brother hasn't returned to his own home.* Erina tapped her brother on his shoulder. He jerked and faced her. "I didn't mean to scare you," she said in a teasing tone.

"I was lost in my own thoughts. I don't often do that."

Lee did act peculiar today. It was out of character for him. Erina gulped before blurting out, "Is there a problem? I sense something's wrong."

He laughed. "I never could fool you. Yes, but it's good."

"Then tell me," she demanded. The wind picked up and pressed against her neck.

He dug his foot into the ground. "Well, I might as well tell you. Put the teapot on and get out those teacakes. I'll tell Adam to join us."

"Alright, " Erina replied.

"Skedaddle!"

Erina rushed toward the porch.

Adam followed her. "I finished the paint in the pail and I'll do more another day. I'd better head for home."

"You'll do no such thing," chimed in Lee while he strode up onto the porch planks. "You're staying here."

"I don't want to impose," Adam insisted.

"You're not," Erina said as she placed her hands on her hips. "My brother wants you here, and that's where you'll be. I'll get the tea going and put out the cakes."

* * *

Adam maneuvered around the small table and sat in the velvet royal-blue settee. He pressed his head against the decorated wooden headrest. He often wondered how this poor family was able to furnish this house with luxuries, such as the sofa he now sat upon. He studied the tall kerosene lamp with its high pottery base with jeweled drop stones. It was one beautiful lamp that no one here could afford.

Erina's brother sat across from Adam in a golden-upholstered armchair. The potbelly stove stood behind him. He raised his face to Adam. "So how do you plan to woo my sister?"

"I – I really don't know." Adam gulped. He had no idea how his facial expressions and actions gave his heart away.

He thought he had hidden those. "What would you suggest?"

"Oh, I don't know what to say. With Mary, I asked her if she wanted to go for a buggy ride." Lee paused. "You might try that. It gives you the advantage of being alone and enjoying the scenery along the way."

"We could do that after church," replied Adam. Doing work around here allowed Adam to see her, but he was outside while she was inside, so her brother's idea was a good one. "A picnic also would be nice. There's a secluded place around a lake close to the church."

"I know the place. Mary and I often went there." He hesitated a few seconds. "Watch out for the boys playing baseball or fishing for they can interfere with your plans." Lee smiled.

"What plans are you talking about?" Erina asked as she stepped into the parlor. Her gaze went from her brother to Adam. She put her hands on her hips. "Just what are you two up to?"

"We're up to no good." Lee laughed.

"I don't like what I'm hearing," Erina replied in a kidding voice. She centered her gaze on Adam. "I can't believe you'd do anything bad. After all, you're a minister."

"I – I," Adam stammered. His cheeks became warm.

"He could be a wolf in sheep's clothing. You never know about some of these preachers," Lee said in a teasing tone.

Erina shook at that thought.

Adam ran over to her and held her for several seconds before he separated from her. "Don't worry, I'll take care of you."

* * *

Her countenance warmed. "You don't have to. I've got Lee to do that." She lifted her gaze from Adam to her brother.

"I won't be able to do much of that for a time," Lee responded. He stared at the parlor's wooden planks.

"Quit looking at the floor. Why can't you help me?" Erina demanded. Her heart pumped heavily in her chest. Her voice rose in agitation. "Explain!"

In slow motion jerks, Lee lifted his head to his sister. "I was going to tell you earlier, but when that clanging came, I ran outside to see what was happening.

"Alright," she replied as she forced her voice calm. "Why can't you help me?" *Is Mary controlling you? Can't you speak up for yourself?* She took several deep breaths. She turned her gaze to Adam. *Can't you do something?*

Adam turned his gaze from her to scan the room. Then he strode to the settee and sat down.

Thanks, she thought sarcastically. "All is ready."

She hastened her steps when she returned to the kitchen. The men shot up and seated themselves at the dining-room table. Erina maneuvered the filled teacups as she steadied her hold on the tray. Once inside the dining room, she set the steaming cups and teacakes in front of Lee and Adam. Erina sipped the hot tea and nibbled on one of the cakes.

"Tastes mighty good," said Adam as he replaced his cup on the saucer and finished his teacake.

Lee grabbed his cup and gulped down a portion of the liquid. "The teacakes are good. You must've learned how to make delicious tea from Ma, for it tastes just like she used to make."

"Yes, Ma taught me her tea secrets." Taking a gulp of the tea, she gazed at her brother, waiting for him to explain why he could not continue to provide the help she needed. A flash of lightning flickered through the double windows. Taking a deep breath, she reengaged her brother. "Now tell me why you can't assist me."

Chapter Nine

Lee glanced up at his sister. He gave her a crooked smile. "I didn't say I couldn't, but for a time, I'll be busy doing other things."

"Like what?" Erina's brow furrowed.

"Like helping my wife."

"With what?" Erina demanded.

"With the baby."

"What baby?"

Lee grinned. "Our child."

"Your child. You mean Mary is in the family way?"

Lee nodded.

Adam stood up, stepped to Lee and shook his hand. "Congratulations!" He grinned. "Now, don't forget to get that lass or lad baptized."

"Will do. Too bad Ma and Pa won't be there." Lee studied his sister's countenance as she stared at her cup. "You all right?"

Erina nodded. "Don't worry. I'll be fine."

Adam inched away from Lee and returned to his dining-room seat. The minister stretched his arm to Erina, waiting for her to grasp it, but she sat there stony-eyed. After a few minutes, he removed his outstretched arm, grasped his teacup and took a sip of the tea.

Trying to break her spell, Lee yelled, "Sis." No answer then he spoke it two more times before Erina jerked up her head.

Erina smiled at her brother. "I'm sorry. My mind was thinking of something else."

"You'll be fine. If I can't do some items around here, you have Adam. He'll be glad to do those for you." Lee grinned.

* * *

I'm sure Adam will, but I don't want him around here. Erina stood up and gathered the saucers and empty cups then placed everything on the tray. She glanced at the double windows. "It looks like it's going to rain."

Lee rose to his feet. "Then I'd better go. I'm sure Mary is back home by now."

"Lee, was Mary telling her mother about the baby, and that's why she wasn't with you today?"

"Yes, we both had to deliver the good news."

Now it all makes sense why Mary wasn't here.

Lee bent down and gave Erina a kiss on her forehead. "Don't worry. It all will work out, and if I'm not here, knock on our door, and I'll come running over here." He paused and added, "Besides, Adam will be checking on you as well."

"Thanks." Erina forced a smile. "Let me know if I can be of some help with the child. I do love those blessings from the Lord."

"I will." Lee gave his sister a hug and dashed out the door.

Erina gazed over at Adam. He still sat at the table.

"Well, I need to be getting home as well." Adam got up then strode to Erina. "I know you don't like me much, but give me a chance. I really have changed." He grabbed the tray from her then strode to the kitchen before he placed the dirty dishes on the worktable near the sink.

Erina followed.

"I better leave now before the rain comes." Adam pretended to sniff the rain. "Don't you love the smell of raindrops on the wet earth?

She giggled. "What rain? It's not coming down now."

"I know, but rain is God's way of showing us His handiwork." He looked down at Erina who stood in front of him. He gave her a crooked smile before he bent down and gave her a quick kiss.

Her lips ached for more. She could barely breathe. Erina squared her shoulders, knowing she could not allow herself to become attracted to her nemesis.

"I'll see you soon." He grinned.

"I – I," she replied, shifting her feet from one to the other.

"Don't worry; I'll take care of you and this place." He studied her countenance.

Her face warmed. "There's a neighbor down the road. I'm sure they would assist me," she said in a soft voice.

Adam gave a hearty laugh. "You mean the Richmonds, who have seven children, and not one is older than nine years old?"

"Um." She cleared her throat.

He leaned over and gave her another quick kiss. "Don't worry. I'll take care of you." Then he raced out the door.

I've got my hands full with him. She put her hands on her hips and observed him descending the hill to get to his family's farm.

* * *

Six-year-old Gertrude Richmond wiggled her short nose against the windowpane. "Ma, the parson is going down the hill." She turned her head to her ma. "Why he up here? Shouldn't he be at church?"

Her ma chuckled. "No, preachers can visit people. Their job is to spread the news of the Bible."

"Oh!" Gertrude shook her head, and her pigtails slapped the back of her neck.

"Parsons also pray with people during troubling and happy times." Ma pulled up a wicker chair and faced her daughter, nicknamed Gerdie.

Gertrude swept her bangs from her eyes and looked at her pretty mother. "Teacher has sad times?"

Her mother nodded. "Everyone has those. Teacher lost her ma a time back."

"That's sad." Gertrude squirmed in her chair. "Where did she lose her?"

"Her ma went to Heaven where the Lord lives."

"Up in the sky?" Gertrude placed her hand on her forehead.

"Yes, Gerdie."

"Can we see teacher's ma like we see the big and little dipper?"

"No, we just know that she's up there." The corners of Gerdie's mother's lips curved up into a large smile.

"How do we know when we don't see her?"

"We just do because Jesus told us about Heaven." Ma took a deep breath.

"If Jesus said that, it must be so." Gertrude smiled. "I love Jesus and I'll pray for teacher and pastor, too."

"You do that."

Gerdie studied her white long apron and examined her saddle-brown boots. She shot up. "I'm happy parson helps people."

* * *

The next day, Adam entered his church office. He needed to write his Sunday sermon. He sat in his wooden office chair and bent over his small desk. He flipped through his leather-bound Bible to get ideas. Nothing caught his attention. His mind returned to the day before when he was with Erina.

Her beauty awed him. He pictured her lovely freckled face with those ocean-blue eyes and those auburn pigtails, which crested each shoulder. He shook his head. *I've got to get working on my sermon.* However, the more he sat, the more his brain twirled with no ideas coming to mind. He fidgeted in his seat. Finally, in disgust, he plopped the pencil down and stood up. *I'll take a walk. Perhaps that will do it.*

He strode out of the church. The spring day greeted him with a blast of warm air. He was determined to stroll around a while before looking for a quiet and cooler place to sit underneath a tree. He inhaled and proceeded with his walk.

"Anyone out there? I need help!" A child's voice shouted.

Adam bent his head to the voice. It came from the north. He looked around but could not see anything. Taking several steps, he shouted, "I don't see you. Yell once more!"

No one responded. His heart beat faster. *This child is in trouble, and I don't know how to get to him.* He prayed, *Lord, help me find this child.* He continued to step north and kept calling to him. No response. His foot slipped on a slick rock and down the reverend went into a ravine. *How am I going to get to that boy now?* Adam planted his feet into the moist ground, grabbed the branch of an offshoot tree and propelled himself upward. He shouted again, "Where are you?"

"Down here," the faint voice replied.

Adam jerked his head toward the sound. One step at a time, the parson maneuvered to the stream's bank. He spotted the boy. The child lay in the water's muddy banks and could not pull himself up. If he stuck out his hand to lift the boy upward, the child's slick muddy hands would land the minister in the mire. *How can I get him out?* Adam asked the Lord.

It was then the parson remembered the large handkerchief he had put in his suit's pocket. The minister pulled it out, shook it open then wiped his moist hands. "Don't move! I'll get you out."

He examined the area around the boy. By standing on the right side of the mud, he could settle his feet securely on hard land. He presented the cloth to the child. "Wipe your hands so I can pull you out."

The boy nodded, wiped his hands and held it up for the minister to take.

Adam bent over the child and, with a firm grasp of the boy's hand, he propelled the child out. "You alright?"

"I'm fine. Thank you. Thank you," the boy uttered. "You my saving grace."

"You could say that, but the real saving grace was the Lord."

"I guess."

"I see. We'll talk more about that later. Follow me to my church, and we'll clean you up there. Got a pump outside."

"Your church?" He rubbed his dirty hands on his britches.

"Yes, I'm the minister at Cross Lutheran."

"Ma ain't going to like that." His curly carrot-topped hair bobbed as he shook his head.

"She isn't going to like seeing you like this," Adam replied, as he studied the child's dirty smudged face and filthy clothes.

"Um, okay."

Adam smiled. He needed to know more about this boy. *What's his name and who are his parents?*

Chapter Ten

The two strode to Adam's church. He turned to the boy. "Now, tell me how you ended up near that river bank?"

"I was fishing. Had me a pole and a darn good-sized fish. I pulled it up, but the bank was wet from last night's rain, and I slipped and fell. I had nothing to pull me up. Everything's wet."

"What about the fish?"

"He got away since the pole landed in the water. Ma looked forward to fish tonight." The boy shook his head. "She'll not be happy with me brunging nothing back to eat."

"I understand. Well, we'll have to see what the church pantry has." Adam glanced at his companion. *He seems like a nice kid. I wonder why his mother hates Christ.* "

They hiked up the hill and now made their way downward. The path ahead of them included bushes, fallen limbs, rocks and rows of cottonwood trees. He turned to the boy. "Do you love spring like I do?"

The child nodded.

A cottonseed swooped down and rested on the pastor's head. He shook his head and laughed. "Of course, I don't appreciate them landing in my hair."

The carrot-topped boy chuckled.

The minister stepped over a series of rocks. The child followed. The church stood in front of Adam and the boy. "I'll go inside and grab some rags to clean you up. You stay here."

"All right."

Adam smiled. "By the way, what's your name?"

"Name's Cliff Gregory."

"Where you live?" the parson asked.

"About a mile down the road," the boy replied.

The preacher strode to his church office, opened a desk drawer and grabbed several rags. He rushed out the door and lowered the well bucket before he wound it up. Then Adam dipped one of the cloths into the pail's cold water. He rubbed the rag into the boy's matted hair. Slowly, he scrubbed Cliff's scalp as the child squirmed. Adam stopped then examined the boy. "Looks good." The parson dipped a different rag into the bucket and presented it to Cliff. "Here, you do your own face."

The boy rubbed and then did his neck. "How do I fare?"

"Clean as a whistle but your clothes are something else."

"Ma ain't going to like that since she washes clothes on Mondays, and today is Monday. She has told me over and over that she don't cotton to church going ever since God took her husband and my pa and left her to tend to five young'uns, including me. If the Lord cared, he wouldn't have done that. She believes."

"I see." Adam studied the boy, wondering what to do. *Can't send him home like this.* He scratched his head. Then he thought of the extra suit, shirt and tie he had in the cloakroom. He kept them there in case a visitor needed proper church clothes to wear. His lips curved up into a smile. "Well, I've got an extra suit, shirt and tie for you to wear."

Cliff shifted his feet before his gaze met the preacher's. "Ma ain't going to like that, but can't go like this, so she'll have to . . ."

"Tolerate it," the preacher chimed in. He nodded and guided the boy to the cloakroom.

* * *

Never had Cliff worn a suit and tie. He liked the feel of the pressed shirt and charcoal-gray suit coat and pants. Although the trousers were a little baggy, the suspenders kept them up just fine. He grinned. "I've not worn something so fine." He glanced down at his dirty shoes. "Sure wish I had better shoes. Makes the suit not look good."

"Understand. Take your boots off, and we'll see if we can clean these up with a brush I have."

"I – I can't do that." Cliff's face warmed.

"Why?" Adam answered in a baffled voice.

He shook his head. "I can't. Ma won't approve."

"She don't need to know," retorted the minister. "I'll get the brush and you take off those shoes."

Cliff stood stoic. His innards churned.

The minister returned with his long, wooden horsehair brush, but the boy did not remove his boots. "Son, I insist you take off those boots so we can clean them up."

"I can't." The boy's voice broke.

Adam's forehead creased. "Sit down in that chair and take them off," he demanded.

The child did not budge. "You don't understand. It's embarrassing. If Ma hears about it, I'm in trouble."

"Sit down, Cliff," Adam spoke in an exasperated voice. "I'll talk to her. It'll be fine."

Cliff relented and sat down in the wooden straight chair. He tugged at his right boot, and it landed on the floor before he removed his left boot. It fell and the cardboard inside fell to the floor. Eyes misty, he reached for the piece on the floor planks. "See?"

The minister laughed. "Cliff, I used those in my shoes as well to plug the holes in my shoes' sole."

"You did?"

"Sure, but we'll both keep this quiet." The preacher brushed the boots. "Much better."

Cliff nodded.

* * *

Adam strode alongside Cliff as they made their way to the boy's house. "Don't worry. I'll tell your ma what happened to you, and why you're wearing a suit and tie. He glanced at his companion and smiled. "It's going to be fine."

"Hope so," the boy responded with hesitation.

A mud puddle stood in front of them. "Step around it," the parson shouted.

The boy hesitated and glanced at the ground. He maneuvered around it. "Thanks. That's all we need is for me to ruin this wonderful suit."

"You're right." Adam laughed. His mind wandered, thinking about how he would approach the child's mother, not only on the clothing but also on her lack of faith.

Cliff ran ahead of the minister and stood in front of the tiny board-and-batten structure, which leaned slightly to its left.

The boy swallowed hard. "There's my house. It ain't nothing much but it gives us shelter."

The parson stared ahead of him. He took a deep breath. The house was quite small with peeled paint and a rotting front door. Adam stepped forward. Three young children stood outside with faces and clothes smudged with dirt from the bottom of their trousers or skirts to the tip of their hair.

A small child approached Cliff. She smiled and glanced up at her brother. "You," she swallowed hard, "you, all dressed up."

"Yep." Cliff grinned. "You like it, Doria?"

She scratched her dark-ash blonde hair before she skipped around him, examining his attire. "You look mighty fine." She pointed to the preacher. "Like, like that parson behind you." Doria paused. "But, Ma ain't going to cotton to it."

Cliff's face turned crimson.

Adam caught up with Cliff. He whispered in his ear, "Don't worry. I'm with you, and I'll explain what happened and why you're in those clothes."

The boy relaxed as they stepped on the loose wooden planks, which creaked as they entered the dark parlor room. The room included two rocking chairs, a potbelly stove and a kerosene lamp, which rested on a square table. Two small windows on each side of the room brought in a little sunlight. Cliff squinted. Then he shouted, "Ma, I'm here with a guest."

From an adjacent room, Ma hustled in wearing a saddle-brown long-sleeve dress topped with a three-quarter length white apron. Her hair tangled and sweat beads ran down her face. "Cliff . . ." She wheezed as she caught her breath. Then she wiped her brow with the bottom of her apron, which exposed two large holes right in the middle of the dress. "I'm sorry; I'm a mess," Ma said, as she glanced up at the visitor.

Cliff stood in front of his mother. "Ma, this is friend of mine. I met him today. He's, he's a –"

"I'm a parson," Adam stated.

Ma turned from him to her son. "Why you brung him here? You know how I feel about these types."

Cliff nodded then swallowed the lump in his throat.

"I cleaned him up. He fell in the stream and couldn't get up, so I helped him. But he ruined his clothing and needed a bath."

"Why thank thee for that." She put her hands on her hips and studied her son. "I see you got church clothes." She shifted her head to the minister. "I don't know what to say."

"He can keep them. These are extra clothes, so no need to return them." Adam forced a smile, knowing she was uncomfortable with the situation.

She gritted her teeth together before she reengaged her son. "You wear those until we find you new ones."

"They are mighty nice, and I don't know what I would've done if the preacher had not found me." The boy gulped.

Ma took a deep breath. "Thank thee but I ain't a believer."

"Why aren't you?" Adam blurted out. "You know He created the earth and all that is in it."

"Ain't sure about that." The heat continued to bear down on her. She again pulled up the corner of her skirt to wipe her brow.

"Sorry to hear that because without Him in my life it would mean nothing." The preacher looked over at Cliff, whose countenance paled. "You got a good boy. I'm glad to have met him and I'll keep in touch. But before I leave, I would like to lead the child in a prayer. If that's alright with you?" Adam asked as he turned his countenance to Cliff's mother.

"I suppose. Sure don't help me much. My husband died and left me these kids and a raggedy house." She wiped her hands on the apron and exited the room.

Adam tapped Cliff on the back of his shoulder and whispered in Cliff's ear. "She's had a hard life. We'll pray for her and all of you." He then led them in prayer.

* * *

As May approached, Erina opened the china cabinet and pulled out two ceramic rose candleholders. Taking the cloth in her hand, she dusted them off before setting them on the white linen tablecloth. Ma had brought these, and the other lovely items, with her from New York. Erina put one candleholder at the head of the table and the other at the foot and placed a white candle in each.

Pulling out the pink-and-rose decorated saucers and cups from the cabinet, she placed them on the table. Everything had to be perfect to honor the birth announcement of her brother's child. Preacher Adam would attend and lead them in a blessing. *A child is so precious.* She would love this newborn no matter whether it was a boy or girl. Erina smiled as she thought of holding the tiny baby and rocking the sweet infant to sleep. Her heart pumped with excitement. Would she ever experience this godly gift? Erina sure hoped so.

She sniffed the fragrant lilacs lying on the table then picked them up and set them in the small vase decorated with a spattering of peach-and-rose painted flowers. Knock. Knock. Erina strode to the parlor door, leaving the vase behind. Erina swung it open. Her cheeks warmed as she stared directly at the last person she wanted to welcome into her home. "Hello, Adam. I – I didn't expect you to be here so soon."

He chuckled. "Thought I'd help you out."

She swallowed hard and pointed to the vase on the table. "Well, I guess you could help by pumping water into this."

"Glad to be of help." He picked up the vase and strode to the kitchen.

Why did he have to come early? I knew I could tolerate him when everyone was here but alone with him? He better not try to kiss me like he did the last time. She spoke out loud, "Or, or –"

"Or, or, what?" He grinned, carrying in the vase.

"I don't remember. Sometimes I speak and forget what I want to say." Erina placed her shaking hands behind her back to hide her trembling fingers.

He smiled "Do I make you nervous?"

"No! Definitely not!" she retorted.

"Then why are you blushing?" His blue eyes twinkled.

"I – I . . ." She turned to the china's silverware drawer and pulled out a couple of the utensils.

He rushed to her and stood in front of her.

"What are you doing?" she asked then took a deep breath.

"I came over to help you," he said in a laughing voice.

"Why, I'm managing just fine, or are you here painting again?" Erina asked as she continued to pull out the silverware.

He gave her a quirky smile. "No, I'm not finished painting. I should wrap up in the next few weeks. " He lifted her chin to him. "Now that's better," he laughed, "for I can see the glint in your eye."

"You're seeing things," she stammered and wiggled away from him to complete her task. *That man! He hasn't changed one bit, and I don't think he'll ever get done with the painting. It's all an excuse to come here.* But she knew she was taken in by his antics. Could she expel his advances when her heart was becoming attached?

* * *

The smell of freshly baked rolls filled the room as well as the tantalizing apple pie waiting to be eaten for dessert. Each person took a seat at the table. The minister settled in the chair at the head while Erina settled in a seat at the table's foot.

Preacher Adam stood up and raised his goblet. "Now, let's lift our glasses as I propose a toast." Erina, Lee and Mary followed with raising their glasses. "I toast Mary and the child she carries." The glasses clanged then each took a sip of their wine. "Before we eat, I'll say a blessing: 'May the good Lord bless this child and may she or he grow like weeds and fill herself or himself with the love of God. And may God bless the food before us.'"

Lee clapped and those around him did the same. "We're looking forward to having this child, raising him in the Lord and providing the best for him or her."

Adam returned to his seat then dipped his spoon into the potato-and-onion soup before taking a bite of his dinner roll. "I congratulate the chef. This is one tasty meal, Erina."

"Why, thank you, pastor." She blushed.

"Mighty good," chimed in her brother. "Tastes just like Ma's."

Erina looked over at her brother and smiled.

Silence filled the room before Mary spoke. "It is quite tasty." She cleared her throat. "Could you show me how to make this? I need to learn how to make more dishes."

"Would love to. Come over one day next week, and I'll make this again, Erina replied after she took a bite of her warm dinner roll.

"Sounds good. I'll do that." Mary returned to her soup.

Quiet overtook the room until Erina stood up and asked if everyone was through with their meal. Each nodded then she began to gather up the bowls.

The reverend smiled. "Have a seat in the parlor and I'll help Erina clear the table."

"You don't need to –"squeaked Erina.

"But, I'm here to help." He winked at her as he assisted her in picking up the rest of the bowls and the small plates that held the rolls.

The evening ended with everyone returning to the dining-room table to eat a piece of fresh apple pie.

"Just like Ma's. Pie is great," stated Lee. "Now if only that family secret could be exposed, then all would be right."

Erina's countenance turned crimson. "It would bring distain upon the family. That's why I must remain silent."

"I suppose," muttered her brother.

Adam darted around the table and stood behind Erina. He squeezed her shoulders. "Proverbs states: 'Open rebuke is better than secret love.'"

* * *

Erina put the dishes away. All was quiet with everyone gone home, including Adam whom she thought would stay around awhile but left with her brother and his wife. After a time of talk and conversation, the quietness returned. The mantle clock clicked down the time.

She returned to the parlor and sat in the armchair to assess the special evening. It had gone well, except for her brother's mentioning of their family's secret. Once revealed, the community would be horrified. Erina had to keep the unmentionable to herself. That also sealed her fate in never marrying. A tear trickled down her cheek. She wanted children. She wanted a regular life. Erina's stomach began to churn. She took a few deep breaths to calm herself.

Life without marriage and children is what she must resign herself to for the sake of her family's legacy. Erina shook her head. *Well, at least, I'm not in love and I must never fall in love.* Although Adam was attracted to her, she would continue to keep him at a distance. After all, he had been mean to her during her childhood. Even if he had changed, she would put up barriers to protect her heart. Yes, her heart had to be guarded.

Chapter Eleven

Cliff peeked into the minister's office. He observed the reverend reading his Bible and writing notes. The preacher did not look up, so Cliff cleared his throat.

The parson lifted his head and smiled. "It's good to see you." He noticed the boy carried a gunnysack. Adam asked in a chuckling voice, "What you got in that sack?"

"The clothes you lent me. Ma insisted I get these to you. She don't cotton to keeping others' belongings."

"Come on in. You're all cleaned up, I see. Pull up that chair in the corner, and we'll talk awhile."

Cliff scooted the straight chair toward the parson's desk before he sat down. "Can't stay long; Ma got work for me."

"I'm sure. Nice to meet your ma and your siblings."

"Siblings?" Puzzled, Cliff's brow wrinkled.

The preacher laughed. "That means your relatives like your brothers and sisters."

"Oh." Cliff pulled out each piece of clothing from the sack and laid them on the floor. "Ma said for me to say thanks."

"I'm glad I could help." He studied the boy's attire. He wore the same cocoa-brown socks, which came up to his gray knickers and a long-sleeved shirt with a sailor collar. The knickers had a tear in them by the knee, and the sailor collar was ripped. He wished the boy could keep this extra set of clothes, but he knew the boy's ma would be offended at the handout. "How'd you like to earn a few pennies?"

"Why, sure," the boy replied.

The preacher grinned. "What about you assisting me with Sunday services with lighting the altar candles, cleaning up around here and helping me take care of a childhood friend. Her ma just passed away, and her married brother won't be able to do much once their baby comes." Adam paused and added, "You'll wear a white robe over your church clothes. You can keep these clothes and dress at home."

"She won't like that at all. But we could use the money." Cliff wiggled his legs from one side to the other.

Sweat ran down the side of the reverend's face. He pulled out his white linen handkerchief to wipe it then stood up to take off his jacket. "Would it help if I talked to your ma?"

Cliff shook his head. "I'll tell her. She'll want me to work regardless of it being church."

"Alright. Come Saturday afternoon, and I'll show you the ropes for Sunday."

"See you then. I'd better go or Ma's temper will get the best of her." He shot up and stretched out his arm to shake the preacher's hand. He raced out of the office with the gunnysack. His stomach churned, knowing the difficulty he faced with his ma's hatred of God. He knew she would relent in his favor because of the money, but it would be a battle.

* * *

Preacher Adam paced the church grounds. He glanced at his pocket watch. It read three-fifteen. With communion this Sunday, he needed the boy to show up soon, or he would run out of time to get everything ready. Perhaps Cliff's Ma decided against it. Adam shook his head. He could not believe she would deny the boy working to bring in an income. However, people do stupid things.

Adam entered the sanctuary, walking past the wooden-seated pews to reach the altar area. He grasped the altar door where they kept the candlesticks that light the candles.

The church doors creaked open. The parson looked up to see Cliff racing inside.

"You're in the sanctuary. This is sacred ground. No running," shouted the minister.

The boy's face paled. "I'm sorry. Never been in church before," Cliff gasped the words out. He changed his pace from a run to a slow walk.

"Come up here, and I'll show you where the candlesticks, candles and other items are kept." The reverend observed the boy's apprehensive approach. He gestured for Cliff to come to the altar.

The boy stepped up. Face grave, he stood in front of the pastor.

Adam opened the door on the right. "Here is where we keep the altar things. Certain occasions will need particular items, such as for Christmas and other Christian celebrations." He picked up the wood-and-brass candlestick. "You'll use this to light the altar candles and the chandelier ceiling lights. To snuff out the lights, use the brass cup on the candlestick's end."

Cliff nodded.

"We'll practice this now so you can get the feel of it. This will take about a half hour, but you don't light the altar candles until the organist pauses before she plays the last tune before the service begins." He smiled at the boy.

"That's when you march up and light the candles. I'll come after you finish." He presented the boy the candlestick. "Your turn."

Cliff swallowed hard before he took the candlestick. His hands shook slightly then he marched up the aisle, stepped to the altar and pretended to light each candle.

The preacher's lips curved up into a large smile. "Well done, boy. You got it."

Cliff returned the candlestick to the parson.

The preacher smiled. "We've got a white gown you will wear over your church clothes. When you arrive, put on your church robe and light the chandelier ceiling lights."

Cliff's hand trembled. "I don't know if – if I can do this. I don't want to fail you but – "

Adam slapped the boy on his back. "You won't fail me. You'll do fine, son. I've got confidence in you."

* * *

Cliff did not believe him. What the minister laid out was overwhelming. Could he do this? Then another thought came to him. "Preacher, what will I do after I light the candles and wait for the service to end?"

The preacher chuckled. "Why, you'll take off your gown and hang it up on the coat rack outside the sanctuary then stay for the service."

"Stay for the service? But Ma will be hopping mad at me." The boy clamped his lips together.

"You need to stay until the last hymn is sung," chimed in the minister. "Then, you put the robe on once more to put out the lights once I say the benediction."

"She'll not be happy with me having to stay for the whole service. I don't know," the boy added in a soft voice.

"Son, it's going to be all right. We'll take care of it, if or when, that happens."

"How?" stammered the boy.

"God will make things right," he replied as he opened the altar door to return the items to the closet.

Cliff gulped. *How will God make things right?* All he knew was his ma would unquestionably be angry, and he didn't want any more whippings in the woodshed. His butt hurt right now just from thinking about it. His shoulders shook. But he knew he needed to do what the preacher asked or lose the money promised. He took a deep breath and waited for the minister to relay more of the tasks he would do.

Chapter Twelve

The chatter of voices met Erina's ears as she stepped outside the church with her brother and his wife behind her. A nice breeze met them as they looked for a table to enjoy the lemonade and teacakes. They paced back and forth and finally found a table for six underneath a tree. "Let's sit here."

"Looks good, and the tree will protect us from the spring rains," Erina's brother stated. Lee placed his plate and a cup of lemonade on the table then pulled his wife's chair away from the table so she could sit down beside him.

Mary placed her dishes on the table then settled in her seat. She turned to her husband and smiled as he scooted her chair to the table. "Thank you, Lee."

"You are welcome."

Erina bit into the soft, flakey cake. "These are so good. I love teacakes, especially on a nice spring day like today."

"Mary bit into hers. Her face paled. "I can't eat them. I'm sick."

"What's wrong?" Lee asked.

"It's my stomach. It's churning like making butter."

"But they're so good. What's wrong with them? I've eaten four." Erina could not understand her sister-in-law's behavior. *She's such a fussy woman.* Then Erina thought perhaps the morning heat had gotten to her. She took her fan and waved it across Mary's countenance. "Does that help?

"No! You don't understand. I'm with child, and you get sick eating in the morning." She heaved then heaved again. She turned to her husband. "You're going to have to take me home."

"But people will talk," Lee replied with exasperation.

Mary stood up. She tapped her foot. "Take me home! You hear me? I've got to go home, or I'll embarrass all of you!"

"Alright." Lee turned to his sister. "Can you find a way home?"

Erina nodded but wondered how she would return home. Preacher Adam and a boy stood a few feet from her. She did not want to ask for his help, but she was desperate since she did not want to climb up the hill. Thus she waved at her old schoolmate.

He gave her a big smile.

Her stomach sank as he strode over to her with the boy behind him. A few minutes later they stood in front of her.

Adam bent his head to her. "Where are your brother and his wife? I saw both of them a few minutes earlier."

"They had to leave. Mary was sick." Meekly, she raised her head to him. Of all things, she had to humble herself to him. A teardrop dripped down her cheek as she took a deep breath. "I'm going to need a ride home, for I had a restless night sleeping last night. I – I don't suppose you could do the honors?"

"Of course, I'll do that." The preacher's eyes lit up. Then he turned to the boy. "However, I need to talk to Cliff first."

"That's fine. I can wait," she replied in a tearful tone.

"Cliff here is my helper. We became acquainted a couple of weeks ago." The pastor's lips curved up into a small smile. "Let me walk with him a little way, and I'll return to you as quick as possible."

"You promise?" Erina stated in a weak tone.

"Of course. You'd doubt my honesty? You have no reason to, Miss Erina."

Oh yes, I do. How many times during our school days did you promise me you wouldn't play mischievous tricks on me? However, you would do it anyway. She shook her head. He said he had changed, but for some reason, she still doubted his ability to do so.

* * *

Adam escorted the boy down the path toward his mother's house. He turned toward Cliff. "You did a good job today. Come Wednesday, a number of young people will gather and learn about the Bible. They meet at 6 p.m., but you come right after school, and I'll show you your cleaning duties."

Cliff nodded. "I'll tell Ma."

"Good. I'm going to leave you now so I can take Erina home." He took a deep breath as they trotted by where Cliff fell. "You be careful, son, and I'll see you Wednesday."

"Thanks. If you don't mind me saying so, Erina is one good-looking woman," Cliff replied while he hastened his steps toward his home.

The preacher smiled. *Yes, Erina was attractive. Even as a little girl, his heart fell for her.* His feet crunched over several twigs lying in his path. He inhaled the smell of dewdrops, which had fallen on the wildflowers. His mind whirled with ideas of how he could win her over. He knew she did not like his sudden kisses. Yet, he could not think of a better way to capture her heart. The family secret stood in his way. Perhaps, if he could get her to divulge that, he could win her over?

* * *

Erina paced back and forth as she squinted through the sun's rays to see if she saw Adam returning. She hated that, of all people, her childhood nemesis had to bring her home. Although Erina was thrilled with her new nephew or niece to come, she could not believe she was stranded with no one to take her home except Adam. She shaded her eyes once more and then let out a deep breath at seeing a man approach. It had to be Adam.

The man quickened his steps, and soon he stood in front of her. He held his gaze with hers before she glanced at the ground. Adam laughed. "You can't get rid of me that easy."

"I – I wasn't trying to get rid of you," she stuttered.

His grin widened. "You weren't? That's news to me." He chuckled.

"I just need a ride home." *Yes, Lord, but why does it have to be with him?*

"I know." He reached for her hand, held it then led her to his buckboard. He gave her a quick peck on her forehead before he lifted her up into her seat. "You are safe with me."

I don't know about that. Her shoulders shook.

* * *

Adam grabbed the reins and flapped them. The horses moved forward. He glanced at Erina, who sat beside him. His heart ached for her. *If only she would accept me, I'm not the person I was in school.* However, he knew that he had to prove it to her. *No, I'm not the childhood boy of my youth because Christ won my heart. But how do I make her see the change?*

The mellow breeze wrapped around them while Adam stirred the beasts toward her house. He flapped the reins again to make the mounts move faster. The rig rattled while they moved up the hill. He glanced over at Erina, who sat stiff and upright in the seat next to him. Crossing her arms, she attempted to rub her shoulders. He turned to her, "Are you cold?"

"Yes, and I didn't bring a wrap. Too much in a hurry so I left it at home."

He chuckled. "Too much in a hurry to be in my presence, were you?"

"Well no, I came to hear the Word." Her lips spread into a large smile.

"Glad about that. I was just kidding with you. You know that, correct?"

She nodded. Again, she stroked her arms.

I've got to do something. He slipped his one hand down to unbutton his suit jacket. It lay loosely on his shoulders. "Grab my jacket from behind me and slip it over your shoulders."

"You sure? Won't you be cold?" she murmured.

"Men can take cold more than the weaker sex."

"I'm – I'm not . . ." She did not finish her sentence and instead pulled at his jacket. Once securing it, she wrapped it around her shoulders. "Thanks. I appreciate this."

"Are you warmer, now?" he asked as he glanced at her while he took his gaze off the road. A sheep headed for the buckboard. Adam swerved the rig to avoid hitting the animal. He lost control and tumbled toward Erina. The two collided. The rig halted. Adam tried to move his body away from hers, but the rig's slant slammed his body into hers. His heart beat faster. He was so close to her. He barely could catch his breath. "You all right?" he squeaked out while his lips scraped hers.

Adam's body trembled. He could not stop his desire. He succumbed to it and caressed her lips several times with a feverish fever of love. "I love you. I love you," he proclaimed.

* * *

"Stop this right now!" she huffed. "We were classmates. That's all." She attempted to push him away from her.

"I'm sorry. I – I just couldn't help myself." He pushed himself upright. "I'm going to make sure everything is all right with the rig." He stood up and gingerly made his way to the ground. He examined the wheels and did not see any damage. He then studied the horses. They were a little restless. Adam stroked their manes and talked to them in quiet tones. The animals settled down. Taking his seat on the buckboard, he pulled her to him.

She started to pull away from him.

"Don't worry. I want you close in case we have another encounter. In that way, I can protect you."

She shrugged her shoulders and kept her mouth mum. *What possessed him to kiss me when I don't want it?* She touched her warm lips. *Now, lips you quit betraying me. There's not a reason in the world I want to be saddled with him.* Even as her mind said this, Erina knew she was falling for him.

* * *

Cliff hastened his steps as he reached his house. Ma stood on the dilapidated front porch. Her fine brunette hair sprinkled with gray spiraled down the side of her face. She wiped her brow with the back of her hand then leaned on the broom in front of her. Raising her head to Cliff, she shouted, "It's about time you returned home. I've got plenty of work for you. Too bad you had to spend time with God. It don't do no good."

Cliff forced a smile. "Now Ma you know I'm making money working for the church."

"I know, but it's against my beliefs, and they'd better be yours as well," she said in disgust.

He nodded. His stomach churned since agreeing with her was wrong. He liked the parson and members of the congregation. Everyone was nice to him. However, he knew better than to tell his ma.

"Go gather some kindling to start the stove's fire. Still cool in the evenings."

He nodded before he entered the wooded area behind the house. He breathed in the dampness of this morning's dew then marched forward when a squirrel scurried across the grass. *Well, I see you're in a good mood*, laughed Cliff. He took a few more steps and found several twigs and sticks. Gathering these up, he headed for his house.

Chapter Thirteen

Adam slapped the reins so the horses moved forward while the buckboard rocked as it moved up the hill.

Erina grabbed the back of the bench to steady herself. "This is one bumpy ride."

The preacher chuckled before he glanced at her. "You are welcome to squeeze even closer to me. In that way, you could hang on to me instead of the bench."

"I'm fine the way it is." Erina shrugged.

"Alright. But we have a couple of curves coming up, so make sure you hold on to that seat tight."

"I will," Erina muttered.

You're a hard one to crack, but I know God has destined us to marry. The parson flapped the reins. The horses sped up and made the curve.

Erina tightened her grip on the seat, but she could not keep her hold. Her hand slipped, and she ended up sliding further toward Adam.

Adam grinned. "I told you. Now listen to me, whether you like me or not, you're going to have to hang on to me."

Erina shook her head. She swallowed her pride and moved even closer to him. She placed her arm around him then used her left hand to grab the seat.

"That's better. We've got one more curve, and it's coming up. Hold on tight!" Adam yelled while he flapped the reins. The horses sped up.

* * *

Erina sighed with relief as she sat steady in her seat. *Now if we can make it home without further problems.* She gazed at Adam. Her heart fluttered. He was a handsome man with those bright-blue eyes, black hair and bulging muscles. Her heart skipped a beat. If only I could marry, I would love to have children. A tear trickled down her face. *I just can't. When the secret is exposed, it will bring disgrace not only to my family, but it could squelch Adam's career as well.* She shook her head and clamped her lips together. *I just can't put Adam or the family through this. It will destroy all of us!*

She pulled her arm from him and wiggled down the bench. Erina could see the Richmond house. Soon they would be home. *Oh God, thank you. Now I have nothing to worry about.*

* * *

Adam pulled the buckboard onto Erina's property. "Whoa!" The beasts stopped. He jumped down and wrapped the reins around the hitching post. He strode to Erina to assist her down from the plank. *What! What! How did she get down without me knowing?* He looked around and saw her pushing the front door open. *You're not going to slam that door on me!* He raced to her and slipped between her and the door. "The least you can do is offer me a cup of tea after this excursion."

His movements caught her off balance, and she stumbled into his waiting arms. He tightened his hold on her. He embraced her and caressed her forehead with a series of kisses. "Honey, you know we're meant for each other! Quit fighting what the Lord has ordained!"

"The Lord has ordained nothing. He sure hasn't told me about it!" she exclaimed while his feverish kisses mounted her forehead.

"Oh yes, He has or God wouldn't have allowed me to take you home," Adam added.

"Ma died and I had to come home. I must return to teaching this autumn."

Adam laughed. "You won't be teaching this fall because we'll probably be married by then."

Erina reached around him and pushed the door open. She stepped into the narrow hallway.

He followed.

Taking a deep breath, she spurted out, "Please leave! I'm tired and want to take a nap. "

"Is that true or are you afraid of me?" His eyes twinkled as he spoke.

"I'm – I'm not afraid of you," Erina stammered.

"Then a spot of tea would be nice." His gaze met hers.

She hated to give in to his squirmy behavior, but she would make that tea. *Will he leave then?* She hoped we would.

* * *

Adam smiled while he unhitched the beasts and boarded the buckboard. She was a difficult lady to win over, but he was not deterred. He chuckled at the quick kiss he gave her after they enjoyed the spot of tea. He snapped the reins and whistled as he led the horses down the road to his family's home.

Ministers were poorly paid, but they would make it. He knew how to farm, and neighbors and church members would help him. He laughed as he remembered her words: "I'll never marry you. Quit trying. It's no use."

Her resistance to his advances made him more determined to capture her heart. No matter the obstacles, she would be his wife. He glanced at his jacket, which now rested on the buckboard seat. When would he see her again? Church next Sunday, of course, even if he had to go and bring her there.

* * *

Adam settled onto his office chair. He leaned over his desk. His mind wandered between his desire to see Erina and the task of writing his Sunday sermon. He shook his head. *This message isn't going to happen on its own. I've got to concentrate.* The preacher twirled his pencil while his mind continued to meander. He shook, trying to stir up his thought processes. It was then the organist groaned out one of his favorite tunes, "Onward Christian Soldiers."

The preacher smiled as he listened to the tune coming from the sanctuary. Then he stood up and tapped his feet on the floor. He could hear the feet vibrations on the wooden planks. Adam now joined the footsteps of others, who danced to the melody. He smiled before he belted out the words: "Onward Christian soldiers, marching as to war. With the Cross of Jesus going on before, Christ the royal Master, Leads against the foe; Forward into battle See his banners go! Onward Christian soldiers, Marching as to war, With the cross of Jesus going on before."

Curious, Adam listened to the second verse as he made his way to the sanctuary. *I must know who is there besides the organist.* He stepped into the room, and there playing the pipe organ was Miss Pepperdine. Then he shifted his countenance to Cliff before Adam went over to him. "Why, it's good to see you today. I'm glad you came early."

"I'm happy I did for I got to hear the organist practicing that hymn coming through the open windows. It's one of my favorites."

"Me, too. You were down this way before Wednesday services started then?" asked Parson Adam.

"Yes, I was gathering firewood. It gets cool in the evenings, and Ma wanted me to bring some home after tonight's services."

Miss Pepperdine glanced at the two of them before continuing to play the song.

The preacher opened his mouth to sing the last verse. But as he did so, Cliff joined in and a rich sounding duet occurred. Adam belted out the tenor, and Cliff sang bass. The velvet sound flowed out the windows, and one-by-one people gathered inside the church for Wednesday's service.

Never had Adam experienced such a response, not from his sermons or any guest speaker who spoke. The preacher lifted up his eyes toward heaven and praised the Lord for what had taken place.

A song miracle, Adam called it as he and Cliff finished out the last verse: "Onward, then ye faithful, Join our happy throng. Blend with ours your voices, In the triumph song: Glory, laud, and honor Unto Christ, the King: This thro' countless ages Men and angels sin, Onward, Christian soldiers, Marching as to war, With the cross of Jesus Going on before. Amen."

People sat mesmerized. Then a small round of clapping ensued until it became louder. After the clapping ceased, one of the parishioners yelled out, "You've got to do that

Sunday. It not only will bring a crowd, but listeners will be transformed to become followers of Christ."

Miss Pepperdine strode from the organ and stood in front of the minister. "He's right, of course. You've got to do this Sunday. I've never heard such splendor."

Adam looked over at Cliff. *Would Cliff feel comfortable singing in front of the congregation?* A lot depended on his response.

* * *

Cliff pointed his middle finger at his lips. He shrugged.

The minister stepped to Cliff. He faced the twelve-year-old boy. "Do you want to sing together this Sunday?" He whispered to the boy, "It's up to you. You don't have to if you'd rather not.

Cliff's lips quivered. He wanted so to do this, but he worried this event could get back to his ma. That could end his ability to work for the minister. He not only would miss the income, but he had become a follower of Christ. That was something his ma should never find out. He shifted his feet. He gulped. "Let's do it. I've found a love of singing God's message."

"You sure?" asked the preacher.

Cliff nodded.

The room of spectators exploded with several series of claps.

* * *

The parson shook his head. He worried that Cliff's willingness to sing for the church could result in controversy, not because of the congregation, but Cliff's mother might get wind of his church singing. He gulped, hoping against hope it would not get the boy in trouble. Adam took a deep breath as he prepared for Sunday's morning service and his drive to pick up Erina.

Erina's brother sent him a correspondence stating he could not come to church until Mary quit having morning sickness. Adam had smiled and was grateful he would have more time to win over his love. More time together made his lips spread into a large smile. *I'm going to triumph despite Erina's family secret. It can't be as bad as she portrays.*

Adam braced his spine against the buckboard's wooden back plank as he flipped the reins for the mounts to climb the hill. The sun peeked behind the charcoal-gray clouds. *It sure looks like rain. I just hope I can get up there before the drops begin to fall.* The parson tightened his lightweight overcoat around him. Thank God he decided to wear it. He hoped Erina also dressed for the cool and possibly a rainy day.

The horses prodded up the curving road. He only hoped the rain would halt until he reached her house. The sun dimmed further behind the dark clouds. He gulped, knowing he could be facing a thunderstorm. He steadied his hands as he swerved around the second curve. Releasing a long breath, he steadied the buckboard as they approached the Richmond house. *Just a little ways more.*

However, that was not the problem. The trouble may occur on the way down. He took a deep breath and pulled into his sweetheart's residence. He had hoped she would be running out to meet him, but instead he had to hitch the beasts and step up to her door and knock.

Chapter Fourteen

Erina's long tan and white-laced dress rustled as she hastened to the door. She swung the door open wide for the preacher. "I'm sorry. I'm running late. I didn't know what to wear with the sunny morning turning to look like rain."

Adam grinned. "You look beautiful."

"Why, thank you, Adam. That's very nice of you."

He scanned her facial features to the bottom of her dress. "Yes, you look mighty pretty." He paused. "You ready to go? We are running late, and I'm the preacher as you know."

"Yes, I'm aware of that." She laughed. "I left my parasol in the bedroom. I'll be right back." She added, "I like your derby hat."

Adam smiled then nodded as he reached into his breast suit pocket to pull out his gold engraved pocket watch with his initials AM. He gave a light chuckle at the reference AM.

"What are you laughing about?" asked Erina as she stood in front of him. "Am I so frightful?"

"Not at all. You're a lovely woman. No, I glanced at my pocket watch. On the outside of the case, are my initials AM. However, *AM* also stands for morning. "I thought it was kind of funny."

"Yes, it is kind of."

Adam slipped his hand in hers and marched toward the door. "We need to head out to miss the upcoming storm."

She nodded.

He swung the door open wide. The sky had turned midnight black, and a rush of wind pressed against him. Lightening flashed in the dark. He pushed her out the door. "We've got to run if we're going to beat this rainstorm."

She clamped her lips together, wishing she could give him a smart tort for rudeness.

He whisked her toward the buckboard. Another round of lightning flashed followed by the clamor of thunder. He gulped.

The horses groaned then pinned their ears back as Adam approached the steeds. Rain pelted down.

Erina carried her tan parasol, which matched her dress. But as she did so, the wind whipped around her. She attempted to open her parasol but the fierce puff of wind collapsed it. The rain pounded her hair and dress. She screamed, "I'm drenched. I'm drenched." Tears poured down her face.

Adam's derby hat sailed down the roadway. He rushed to Erina and pushed her toward the house. "You go inside. I'm going to put the animals and buckboard in the barn until this calms down."

"But, but we'll be late," she protested.

"We'll have to wait or the buckboard will get stuck in the muddy roadway."

She sprinted to the house while the rain pounded her. Her shirtwaist was soaked and stuck to her legs. Erina could barely walk as she approached the front door. She reached for the doorknob and attempted to open it. However, the rush of wind slammed it shut. Gripping the knob once more, she tried to open it, but another gust of wind banged it back in place. Rain continued to pelt down. Once more, Erina gripped the doorknob. Her hands slipped. Her body shook.

Then all at once, a large hand reached for the door and swung it open. Wet and drenched, Erina darted inside. "Thank you," she whimpered, while she studied the man in front of her. For the first time, she examined her former classmate and saw him in a new light.

* * *

Water dripping, Adam gazed up at Erina. "You look like a drenched cornstalk doll."

"I bet and you don't look any better." She chuckled.

"I know. I'm dribbling water all over the place, and the bad thing is I can't even sit down, for I'll get everything wet."

Erina grinned. "We're in a bad predicament and even smell like wet dirt."

"How are we going to fix it? We can't smell and stand forever while continuing to drip all over."

"You're right." She giggled. "But I have an idea. You go to the dining room, and I'll bring in my pa's farm clothes. He wore 'slop' overalls and there's a shirt as well. I'll bring those to you and you can change out there."

"Alright." He stared at his lovely miss. "What you going to do about that beautiful dress?"

"I've got another church shirtwaist, so I'm fine." A wide smile spread across her face.

"Do you really think we'll make it to church?" Adam asked.

"I don't know, but I'll be prepared in case we can get there before the service ends."

"Without a minister there, I don't know what will happen. The whole church could be empty." Then Adam thought of Cliff. *Oh no, what's going to happen? Will he sing that hymn alone, or will the church service be cancelled which has never occurred?* The preacher stepped to the dining room to await Erina's entrance.

* * *

The rain pelted down as church members arrived. Miss Pepperdine exited the carriage along with her ma. Pa parked the vehicle as the women opened their parasols and ran toward the church.

"I can't believe the reverend isn't here. He's always here awaiting my arrival," exclaimed Miss Pepperdine as she and her ma strode into the sanctuary and folded their umbrellas.

"You're right. It is odd, but this storm could've delayed him," added her mother.

"I suppose but it certainly is weird."

Miss Pepperdine stepped up to the pipe organ. Opening her hymnbook, she placed her hands on the keys and ground out a tune.

Her mother sat down, and soon her father sat beside his wife. Little by little, the small church filled up but not to its capacity. The weather prevented it from that.

Miss Pepperdine tried to smile as she gazed out of the corner of her eye to see if the minister had arrived. *Where is Cliff as well? He and the preacher were to sing that hymn.*

The sanctuary became loud with voices talking. Finally, Cliff arrived. He stepped up to the altar area and took a long breath. He stood beside Miss Pepperdine and inquired about the preacher.

She shook her head and beckoned to Lucas Pierce to come up to the altar. Leaving his wife and their four boys seated, he stepped up to the organist. He leaned over and asked where Reverend Miller was.

Miss Pepperdine shook her head as she continued to play.

Then Mr. Pierce turned to Cliff and asked him the same question.

"I don't know," Cliff replied.

The parishioners became louder as they waited for the service to commence.

Miss Pepperdine whispered to Mr. Pierce, "It's getting late. We've got to start the service. I believe the minister got stuck in this rainstorm. He was to pick up Miss Erina Higgins this morning."

* * *

Cliff stood at the altar podium. He cleared his throat. "I – I know most of you don't know me. Ma, me and my brothers and sisters live up the holler. Our last name is Gregory. We're not churchgoers, but after I met your minister, I became a believer."

The audience smiled up at him.

He took a deep breath. "I believe Reverend Miller got stuck in the rainstorm and couldn't make it back for the service. The parson and I were going to sing, 'Onward Christian Soldiers.'" Cliff swayed back and forth. "The preacher was to do the tenor and I the bass. I – I don't know how to proceed."

Mr. Pierce stepped to Cliff. Then Pierce addressed the congregation. "What about Cliff Gregory singing the words of the hymn, 'Onward Christian Soldiers,' and the rest of the congregation joining Cliff on the refrain?"

"Sounds great," shouted several in the crowd. Others nodded in agreement.

Mr. Pierce smiled. "Then it's all yours Mr. Gregory and Miss Pepperdine." The audience clapped.

Cliff maneuvered to the middle of the altar area then glanced over at Miss Pepperdine. She placed her hands on the keys as Cliff opened his mouth where a low, deep voice with rich tones reverberated around the room. As each word was sung, congregants' eyes widened and large smiles spread across their faces.

Finally, the last verse came: "Onward, then, ye people, Join our happy throng, Bend with ours your voices, In the triumph song; Glory, laud, and honor, Unto Christ the King; This thro' countless ages Men and angels sing."

People stood up raised their hands, clapped and then joined Cliff with the refrain: "Onward, Christian soldiers, Marching as to war, With the cross of Jesus, Going on before!"

Miss Pepperdine rose to her feet then strode to stand beside Cliff. "Please lead us in our hymn singing."

"Yes," shouted the congregation.

"I don't know all the hymns, but I'll do my best." Cliff shifted his feet then smiled. "What do you want to sing?"

"Just as I Am," announced a long-bearded man in the third row.

"What about 'Best Be the Tie that Binds'? A young woman who wore a cream-colored dress shouted.

Cliff chuckled. "Sounds good. We'll start with those and once done; we'll ask for more."

One hymn after another was sung until Mr. Pierce returned to the altar. "I'll conclude the service with the benediction. The Lord bless thee and keep thee. The Lord make His face shine upon thee and be gracious unto thee.

The Lord lift up His countenance upon thee and give thee peace."

Miss Pepperdine ground out the organ's response while the congregation sang amen, amen, amen.

Cliff rushed toward the exit, but each time he took a step a member stopped him and thanked him for his great singing voice. He never had experienced such bliss. Then he gulped, hoping this service would not reach his mother's ears. *She would not be pleased. No not at all.*

* * *

Adam put on the long-sleeved shirt before he slipped on the "slop" overalls. *I pray the good Lord understands why I'm not dressed in my Sunday best.* Out of his trousers, he pulled out his damp handkerchief and wiped his face. Then he placed the cloth in his farmer pants. His wet clothes lay on one of the dining-room chairs while he settled in a seat next to them. Waiting for Erina to return, he stepped to one of the double windows and lifted one of the cotton curtains to see outside. The raindrops still splashed down, but he did not see any lightning nor hear any thunder. "That's good," he spoke out loud.

"What's good?" replied Erina.

He turned to her and grinned. "Why, the rain."

"Has it stopped so soon?"

"No, but the lightning and thunder have." Adam chuckled. He studied his lovely. She now wore a pastel-blue dress embroidered with ivory thread around the neck and high collar. "You look stunning in spite of being a wet cornstalk doll."

"Why, thank you." Erina laughed. "Are you trying to flatter me?"

"Yes." He bent down and kissed her.

For the first time, she responded with warmth.

I'm breaking through. I'm breaking through. She will become mine. She will become mine, while he continued to caress her lips. Finally, he pulled his from hers. She stood there trembling. Erina wanted more.

He wanted to abide with her desire, but he knew it could get out of hand, so he kept his distance. He maneuvered again to the windows. Adam knew what he wanted, but good propriety told him to keep his inflaming desire to himself. "Rain still is pouring down. What shall we do while we wait for it to stop?"

Face flushed, she took a deep breath. "Why, I could fry some bacon and eggs. I also could cook some porridge." She sighed then asked, "How does that sound?"

"It sounds grand. Coffee?"

"Of course." Erina smiled before she stepped into the kitchen.

Adam followed.

* * *

Erina placed the pink-and-rose cereal bowls, piping with porridge, on the dining-room table.

Adam dug into the cereal. "Tastes mighty good."

"Why, thank you."

She then fried the eggs and bacon and put those on the china plates. Erina bent down and placed Adam's food in front of him. "Now eat hearty," she said.

"You bet. How could I otherwise with the smell of bacon peaking my appetite," he replied while he aimed his fork at the eggs and took several bites before jumping up and bumping into Erina. "Sorry, I got up to get the salt and pepper shakers." He held her in his arms then he caressed her lips. From there, he inched up to her earlobes and kissed them before he planted a large kiss on her brow.

She melted in his arms. Secretly she wanted more, but she could not let him know that. After all, he was a parson, and there could be no scandals, or he could lose his position and the respect he enjoyed.

"Oh, sweetheart, I love you." His eyes twinkled.

"I know," she murmured. "I – I don't know what else to say."

"Say, you love me." He brought her to him. He kissed her feverishly.

Her resistance evaporated. She hung to him like clothespins on a clothesline. Her body trembled with desire. *I have to get him to stop, or something bad will happen.* Her mind searched for a word or words that could end this encounter. She gave a soft laugh and glanced at the stove. "The coffeepot is steaming. It's going to boil over."

He lessened his hold on her.

Trembling, she took a long breath, straightened her back and dashed to get the coffeepot.

Adam grabbed the shakers and returned to his seat. He took another bite of his egg and crunched on a piece of bacon as Erina approached and poured the hot coffee into his cup. "Sit down and eat. I want you beside me."

She obliged, placing the pot beside her plate and began to eat her breakfast.

The preacher stood up.

What's he doing? I thought he wanted me to sit by him. Her brow creased in puzzlement.

Then he poured the coffee into her cup. "See, I can do some women things."

She chuckled. *I'm falling in love with him. What am I going to do?*

Chapter Fifteen

His stomach full, Adam separated the dining-room curtains to look outside. "The rain has stopped," he shouted to Erina, who was in the kitchen.

Carrying a dishtowel, she ran into the dining room. "What did you say?"

"The rain has stopped," he repeated.

"Why, that's good. What about the roads?"

"They look muddy, but I think they'll dry up pretty quickly with the sun out. Did you take care of Daisy and gather the eggs?"

Erina shook her head.

"I'll do it while you finish up."

"Thank you."

He stared at his love. Her auburn curls fell down the side of her face. Her luscious lips curved up into a sensuous smile. He could not resist and marched toward her. Standing in front of her, he placed his wet lips on hers and caressed them for several moments.

She went limp.

He knew he had won her over and stopped before it became too heated. "I'm leaving now. You finish up in the kitchen."

"Alright." Erina headed to the kitchen.

Adam stepped outside. He sniffed the fresh smell of raindrops. It energized him as he headed for the chicken coop. He may not have been able to preach his message, but he sure made headway with his former classmate. *She's beginning to love me. I'm making progress.* The minister smiled. *But, it's all in the Lord's hands.*

* * *

Miss Pepperdine tidied up the music around the organ before making her way out of the church. She raced after Cliff, wanting to congratulate him on his singing. Could she reach him in time? She wanted to see if he wanted to participate in the area churches' musical contest where they would compete with other singers in June. The talent show could use a rich and deep voice like Cliff's. Her feet stumbled as she stood near him. She reached out her arms, but as she did so, she plopped to the ground. Mud oozed over her shoes and on her new pantaloons and shirtwaist.

Cliff reached down and pulled her up. He grinned at her. "You look a little messy."

"A little?" She gave a light chuckle before she shook her head in order to clear her blonde hair of the sticky mud stuck to her locks. Miss Pepperdine inhaled the rain-soaked earth before she raised her head to the boy. "I'm going to have to clean up, but before I find my parents, I wanted to ask if you would be interested in participating in the area's church singing contest in early June."

"Not in the least. My ma would whip me for doing something like that." He took several steps away from pretty Pepperdine.

"But – but you've got such a wonderful voice," she begged. "Besides, the competition could earn you fifty dollars." Miss Pepperdine folded her arms.

"I – I can't. Ma doesn't know I sang here today, and she wouldn't be happy."

"Oh! Forget that. Think of the money you could receive," she snapped.

He scratched his scalp. "Could use the money, though. But if Ma found out, she would never forgive me."

"Why?" Miss Pepperdine's jaw opened wide.

"Because she hates God and blames Him for taking our pa at such a young age."

"Oh, that's terrible." Miss Pepperdine pulled out her fancy cloth from her skirt's pocket to dab her eyes. Black mud caked around her eyes. "Jesus died so we can live in glory with Him. He will help her get through this."

Cliff gulped, "I know you're right but Ma won't."

"Think about it. Fifty dollars would do a lot to help," she replied as Cliff stepped away from her. She would approach him again. *After all, the competition still was several weeks away.*

* * *

Adam returned to the church. The soaked ground had dried up from this morning's outpour. He lit a candle and entered the sanctuary. Dampness in the air entered his nostrils as he paced the church floor. He did not know why he stopped here instead of going straight home, but the Lord urged him to do so.

A low crying voice alerted his attention. He paused and turned his candle to the sound. There sitting in the second pew was five-year-old Doria. Tears dripped down her cheeks. The preacher took a deep breath before asking, "What's wrong? Can I help?"

She shook her head. "My brother, Cliff, is going to get in trouble."

"Why?"

"Because he's got God in his heart."

"Why, that's a good thing, child." Adam gave a low chuckle.

Dorie shook her head. "No, it's not because Ma don't like God. He took my pa."

"I'm sorry. I know it's rough without him." The preacher hugged her. "But God will take care of you. Don't forget that."

"Even – even if I don't believe?" Her words came out like a whisper.

"Let's bow our heads in prayer." He tightened his grip on her delicate hand. "Here is a child of God, and she's scared her brother is going to face dire consequences for believing in You. Help her realize that no matter what happens you will get the family through this. You are in control, and you will wipe their tears away."

She sighed and pulled out a small, delicately laced handkerchief.

He did not release her until she wiggled from his grasp. He turned to her. "Let me walk you home."

"I don't know. Ma might see you, and you and me would get a tongue-lashing."

"Don't worry. When I see your house, I'll let you run to it, and I'll return to the church."

She nodded.

"Remember the Lord is there with us, and we'll be fine." He observed her running toward her house, and once the door shut, she did not reappear. Adam turned around and headed back to the church.

* * *

A few days later, the parson sat in his church office when Cliff sheepishly stepped into the room and pulled up a chair in front of the minister. Cliff cleared his throat as Adam looked up from his Bible and smiled. "Good to see you. Everyone loved your singing this last Sunday. You ready to do that again tonight and Sunday?"

"I – I don't know," Cliff stammered.

"Why? God gave you such a gift."

"I – I know but I'm afraid my family will find out, and I don't want to hurt my ma. She's all I have."

"Yes, I know." The minister stood up and stepped to Cliff. He placed his hand on the boy's shoulder. "You think about it and ask the Lord for direction."

Cliff examined the wooden floor beneath his feet. "I love the gift God gave me, but if Ma found out, it would be devastating."

"It could be, but when the Lord is in control, you never know what will happen."

Lifting his head up, Cliff's brow furrowed.

"Son, it's your decision. Pray about it. The Lord will guide you. Take your time and get back with me. However, don't forget the deadline for becoming part of that competition. It is in a few weeks, thus you'll need to come up with an answer before that." Adam released his hand from Cliff's shoulder.

* * *

Cliff stepped out of the church. He had found the Lord there and it made him whole. *For years, I felt empty inside, but now I am happy and full of joy. God, you made the difference.* His stomach churned. What should he do? *If I stay with the church where I found peace, Ma will find out.*

Someone will tell someone, and it will spread like wildfire that I became a Christian. Cliff sniffed the cool air as he strode the grounds. He did not want to go home because his ma would wonder why he was not at Wednesday night services.

With the cool spring air circulating around him, Cliff headed for the stream where he and Rev. Adam Miller first met. There he could think in quiet. The sun had dried up Sunday's rainstorm. He stepped down to the water and sat on the bank. He raised his face to the darkening sky, which calmed him. Frogs croaked. As a child, he never took time to realize the beauty around him. The water stirred as the fish splashed. He breathed in the fishy smell, but the whole scene relaxed him.

He reached for a pebble beside him and threw it into the water. Ringlets formed. He could stay here all night but knew he must return home. The peacefulness settled his anxiety. There was no answer but the one deep in his heart. He had to do it. Cliff had no choice.

Chapter Sixteen

Erina woke up after a restful sleep. This was the first morning she had not mourned over her mother's death. She stretched her arms above her head to fully wake up. The fresh air sweeping through the room gave her comfort. She had opened the bedroom windows for the first time last night. The cool spring had departed, and the late spring brought warmer temperatures and more sun. Easing the cinnamon-and-pink quilt from her shoulders, she pushed herself upright and yawned.

Taking a deep breath, she danced around the room then opened her mouth to sing the hymn, "When Morning Gilds the Skies. My heart awaking cries, May Jesus Christ be praised! Alike at work and prayer, To Jesus I repair; May Jesus Christ be praised."

Erina straightened the creases in the sheet then she grabbed the edges of the bedspread and pulled it over the pillow. She smiled before she sang the last verse: " To God, the Word, on high, The hosts of angels cry, May Jesus Christ be praised! Let mortals, too, up raise, Their voice in hymns of praise, May Jesus Christ be praised! Amen."

She stepped to the dresser and picked up the water pitcher before pouring its contents into the basin. Erina dipped the cloth into the cool water then dabbed the wet liquid over her face and underarms. The cold water made her shiver. She slipped on the navy-blue calico dress with lace around the neckline with its three-quarter-length sleeves. Erina smiled while she looked into the dresser's mirror. *Yes, this is the perfect outfit for today.*

Why am I so happy? Then she thought of Adam and how much she liked the man. He had redeemed himself to her. A thought hidden curled up inside her. *But I haven't fallen in love with him? No, I'm not in love with him. I'm – I'm . . .* She could not finish the sentence, for she knew she could not marry with the secret swirling inside her. The scandal to her brother, to Adam and all who stood with him would make their lives unbearable. She must not fall in love.

No matter how difficult, she needed to keep their relationship at a distance because she knew the secret would ruin them. Erina took a deep breath. For now, she could see him sparingly. Tears filled her eyes. *What's wrong with me? Perhaps you love him.* She shook her head. "No, no I don't," she shouted, as droplets fell down her face.

* * *

Adam sat in his church office, thinking of Wednesday's night service. Cliff's absence last night made everyone sad. His bass voice and the emotion he put into his singing lifted the congregation's spirits, but without him there, the service went flat. He hoped this interlude would be short, but he did not know. *Whatever, the boy needs to make a decision.*

He opened his leather Bible and it fell to this verse, Proverbs chapter three, verses five to six: "Trust in the Lord with all thine heart; and lean not unto thine own understanding. In all thy ways acknowledge him, and he shall direct thy paths."

That's perfect! Thank you, Lord. The parson stood up and exited his office. He stepped outside and looked over at the peony bushes near the church entrance. The beautiful blooms were in white and rich pinks. He smiled. *Erina would love this.* His lips curved up into a large smile. *I'll cut some and take them to her this morning.*

He headed for the church, opened the sanctuary altar door and retrieved the scissors. He cut several blooms and put them in a wet newspaper. *I must go to see her now or the flowers will die.* He laughed. He knew *his love* would appreciate them.

He raced to his family farm and creaked open the barn door to retrieve the buckboard. *Erina is going to love this. I just know it.* "Giddy up! Horses. Giddy up!"

The steeds clomped up toward the hill of his sweetheart.

* * *

For the second day in a row, her brother failed to gather the eggs. She knew this because she did not hear the chickens clucking, and they would if someone was inside. Her brother was bound to assist Mary, but all this made it difficult for Erina to take care of the house inside. Curtains, linens and dirty laundry all needed to be cleaned. She had set today for doing these, and she was determined to get those done in spite of having to do her brother's chores.

Her heartbeat sped up. She took several long breaths to calm herself. *Where was Adam when she needed him?* Erina headed for the chicken coop.

The hens clucked as Erina grabbed the egg basket. *I hear you. Did you miss me?* She smiled. Two hens flapped their wings in the excitement. She sprinkled an assortment of grains and table scraps for the chickens. Slipping her hand into the nests, she grabbed the saddle-brown eggs and put them in her basket. Then she unlatched the door and stepped outside.

Wheels rattled. Erina turned her head toward the noise. She strode to the buckboard. Standing in front of Adam, she grinned. "What you doing here?"

"I came here to bring you something special." Adam smiled. He stepped down from the vehicle with his right hand behind his back.

"What's behind you?" Erina chuckled.

"Something special." His eyes twinkled. "You take your egg basket inside, and I'll follow you."

She nodded and strode to the house with Adam following.

Unloading the eggs into a large bowl, she turned to him. "Alright. Now show me what you have."

"I've got something special," he replied in a teasing tone.

"I know. You already said that." The corners of her lips curved up into a smile. "Now show me."

He laughed and stood there with his hand still out of reach.

She tried to grab it.

He maneuvered away from her.

"Come on!" She extended her arm toward him. As she did so, she lost her balance and ended up inside his arms. An object grazed her arm. She glanced down at the blooms. "You brought me flowers."

"Yes, sweetheart." He caressed her lips. "I'll give these to you if you pucker up for another kiss."

"You're hopeless." Erina giggled in spite of herself.

He caressed her lips.

Her body slumped inside of his arms. *Oh no! I can't fall in love with him. I have to keep the family secret.*

* * *

"I hate to stop the kissing, honey, but I'd better finish the chores. I'll go milk Daisy while you make 'your-husband-to-be' breakfast," Adam said in a teasing tone.

"Who said 'your husband-to-be;' I never—never agreed to that," she stammered.

His lips curved up into a large smile. "Are you sure about that?"

"Yes," she cried in defiance.

He wrapped his arms around her once more and caressed her lips to the tips of her earlobes.

She melted in his arms.

"See, I told you I'm your husband-to-be.' After all, you just proved my point."

"How?"

"By enjoying those kisses of mine." He smiled and left the house.

* * *

That man is so aggravating. Erina opened the icebox and grabbed several pieces of bacon before she dropped them in the pan. The meat sizzled. The smell was tantalizing. *Oh, I can cook and keep house, etc., but I don't know how to prevent Adam from coming around.* Pulling out a small lavender and white flowers decorated plate Erina placed the bacon on it. *It smells good enough to eat.* She giggled.

With the grease still hot, Erina cracked the eggs then dropped them in the frying pan. She scooped them up and placed three eggs on Adam's plate and put one on Erina's.

She inserted the bread into a wire contraption with long handles. Once done, she placed one toast on his plate and the other on hers.

As Adam stepped into the dining room, Erina strode to the coffeepot and poured the hot liquid into the cups. She lifted her face to him. "Well, all is ready." She settled herself into a chair opposite him. She bent her head, waiting for him to say the blessing. She sat there waiting, waiting. Raising her head to him, "You going to say the blessing?"

"Of course." He laughed. "I thought you were going to do the honors."

"Me?" she squawked.

"Why yes, you're the one who had *her* head bowed."

"But you're the preacher," she responded.

He nodded. "I am but you had your head bowed."

"All right, say it!" Erina's voice got louder.

He lowered his head. "Thank you, Lord, for this wonderful breakfast and for the person sitting opposite from me, my future wife."

Her countenance became heated. She ate as fast as she could. *What makes him think I'm going to marry him? Yes, I'm falling in love with him, but I can't. The secret. The secret. I can't reveal the secret.* Then her mouth opened and spurted out, "I can't fall in love with you. The secret. The secret."

He rushed to her then caressed his lips on hers. "Oh, sweetheart, you can't keep this inside. In Matthew, it states in chapter six, verse six: 'But thou, when thou prayest, enter into thy closet, and when thou hast shut thy door, pray to thy Father which is in secret; and thy Father which seeth in secret shall reward thee *openly*.'"

Erina covered her eyes and muttered through her tears, "What should I do, dear Lord?" She reached for Adam's hand and held it tight.

* * *

Adam held her hand and squeezed it. *Oh Lord, I don't know what to do. She needs to release this secret to you or this will eat at her insides.* His strong hands trembled as he released his from hers. "Erina, talk to the Lord. He will guide your path."

"But, but …" she stammered.

"Erina, take deep breaths and give this problem to Him. You can't continue to keep this inside. The Lord will guide you." Adam returned to his seat. He ate his meal fast. He wanted to stay to comfort her; however, on the other hand, he believed she needed to be alone. The parson cleared his throat. "Perhaps I need to leave so you can think." His voice became mellow.

She nodded. Then all at once, tears streaked down her countenance. "I – I want you to stay. I don't think I can do this by myself. I need you. Do you have to return to the church?" she cried.

"No, pastors are known for helping people through their troubles. The Lord can heal all wounds."

"Thank you," she muttered.

Adam reached for her hand once more and stroked it. "You're shaking, darling."

"I know. I know," Erina responded. Her eyes were downcast.

"Take deep breaths. Remember the Lord is with you."

She took several deep breaths. Her fingers quit quivering. "I'm doing better now."

"That's great, honey." He fell on his knees.

"What are you doing?"

He grinned. "You need someone strong like me. I love you. I will take care of you. I did not plan for me to ask you to marry me today. But the Lord directed my path, and I've been carrying this little square box for a month. You need my loving support." He reached inside his trousers and pulled out the box. "This was my grandmother's ring. It's a European cut with a diamond in the middle and diamond accents around it. My grandmother wore it until my grandfather passed away. Then she returned it to the box. 'Must keep it pretty for a young lady, my grandmother said.'" He placed it on Erina's finger.

She smiled. The antique white diamond shined as she rotated her fingers. "It's so pretty. Are you sure of your feelings?"

"Yes." He stood up and caressed her cheeks."

"But I'm such a mess. Are you sure?" she asked in a whimpering voice.

"I will stand beside you no matter what. I love you."

* * *

"I love you, too but did not realize it until now." She stared at the sparkling ring. "It sure is pretty. I'm happy to wear it. Thank you," she replied, her voice almost a whisper.

"Happy you like it, and I'm engaged to the most marvelous woman ever!"

"Me too, except I'm engaged to the most marvelous man ever!" Erina dabbed at her eyelids with her laced cloth.

He stood up and gathered up the dirty dishes.

She followed him to the kitchen and scraped the residue from the plates before putting them in the dry sink. She bent her head down to clean them.

He stood behind her and began kissing her neck.

"What are you doing?"

"It's called necking."

"Necking? I didn't know parsons did such things," she responded in a teasing tone.

"Well, I'll have you know they do, especially after the lady accepts his proposal."

"I don't believe . . . You made this up." She laughed. "I can't believe anything you say."

He turned her around. "Honey, you can believe I love you, and we will fight the battles ahead for the Lord will stand beside us." He caressed her forehead, moved down to her nose and kissed her luscious lips.

She became limp inside his arms.

He tightened his arms around her and steadied her. "When the Lord is with us, we can conquer whatever tries to destroy us."

She had succumbed. "No matter what ails us, God will steer us!"

He nodded.

She shook her head in agreement and surrendered her heart to the Lord.

Chapter Seventeen

Cliff shuffled toward the church. He squeaked open the church door. He took a deep breath as he strode toward the minister's office. *Keep your voice calm. Steady yourself.* After reaching the minister's office, Cliff tapped on the closed door. No answer. *That's odd.* He knocked again. Still no answer, Cliff creaked the office door open. There he found the parson bent over his Bible.

He strode to him. Cliff cleared his throat, hoping to wake up the minister. The parson did not stir. Cliff cleared his throat once more. "Pastor Adam, are you awake?"

The parson's eyes flickered then shut.

Cliff clasped his right hand over Adam's left.

The minister's eyes flew open. He darted his attention around the room before Adam returned to focus on Cliff. "I'm so sorry. I fell asleep. I've been helping Erina around her place, and I guess that and doing the church duties I'm just plain wore out." He grinned. "And yes, we're engaged. I presented her my grandmother's ring last week."

Cliff grinned.

The preacher took a deep breath. "Well, what did you decide to do about the voice competition?" He locked eyes with Cliff.

"My heart is with the Lord, so I must do it regardless of the consequences with my ma."

"I'm proud of you." The parson stretched out his hand and squeezed Cliff's before he pulled his hand from the boy's. "How about we go for a walk? I need to sniff the rest of the spring air before summer arrives."

"Sure." Cliff stood up. He smiled. "The competition is coming up in the next weeks." He gulped. "Could I practice here? I've already asked Miss Pepperdine to accompany me on the piano, and she told me to come early Wednesday night to practice."

"Of course, the whole church is pulling for you to win." The parson rose and the two of them stepped outside. "What did you decide to sing?"

"One of my most beloved hymns, 'Amazing Grace.'"

"Everyone loves that tune," replied the preacher.

"I know. It reaches your heart." Cliff stopped and pointed at the cardinal ahead, resting on a tree branch. "He's singing his rich tunes, one after another. Must've found a pretty young female to mate." He laughed then opened his mouth, and in his deep bass voice, he sang, "Amazing grace! How sweet the sound, That saved a wretch like me! I once was lost, but now am found, Was blind, but now I see."

"Oh, that's perfect because you were lost and now are saved, and your voice brings witness to those who hear you." The parson strode through the tall wet grasses as they passed the tree with the bird."

"Thanks. I thought the same." Cliff sniffed the moist air while he continued to strut down the worn path. "The voice competition is at the Presbyterian church several miles from here. The church has a good organ and piano, and Miss Pepperdine can play for me." He stopped a minute and took a deep breath. "I'm looking forward to winning the fifty-dollar prize. That would help Ma a lot."

"Sure would. How will they judge the contest?" asked the preacher while he stepped over a large rock.

"Clapping. The audience decides by that." Cliff took a deep breath to calm his nerves. The more he talked about it; the more nervous he became. "I'm getting anxious and am afraid my bass will sound like a shrill train whistle."

The parson laughed. "We'll make sure that doesn't happen."

But how? Cliff pondered.

* * *

Miss Pepperdine sat on the piano's bench. She smiled as Cliff approached. "You ready for the rehearsal?"

He nodded.

"You sure? You look peaked."

He cleared his throat. "Just got a tickle in my throat. I haven't been able to get rid of it."

"Sip on hot tea. That seems to fix whatever ails a person. The last week of May had brought colder temperatures, and that may have given you this tickle."

Cliff nodded then pulled out his large handkerchief and wiped his brow. "I just ain't feeling well. I'm sorry." His shoulders shook.

Miss Pepperdine ran down to meet Cliff and examined his hot cheeks. "You look horrible. The competition is in a couple of weeks. Do you want me to take your name off the Tekamah list?"

"No, let me see how I'm feeling," he answered in a hoarse voice.

The cooler air circulated through the sanctuary's open windows. Miss Pepperdine shivered. "Need to close those windows. That's not helping you or me."

"I'll close them."

Miss Pepperdine gazed up at Cliff. "You're in no condition to do that."

"I'll be fine. You shut those two side windows at the end, and I'll do the others." He rubbed his cheeks with his hands then strode to the windows and creaked them down. Cliff lost his balance.

"I've got to get you home. You're too sick to walk the distance."

"I'll be fine. Don't worry." He shook once more.

"But, look at you. I can't let you do that," Miss Pepperdine cried. She ran out of the church, took her handkerchief and cranked the well rope to pull up the bucket. Once up, she dipped her cloth into the cold water and rushed into the sanctuary. Without the windows open, only a streak of light illuminated the church. "Where are you Cliff?" she yelled. No response. The silence was deafening. Her heart thundered in her chest. *He's got to be in here somewhere.*

She continued to search and holler for Cliff. *Where is he?* She gulped then she saw a glimmer of light. She sprinted to it. Cliff's golden-cased pocket watch shimmered in the darkness. He lay on a middle pew. She shook him. "Cliff, Cliff," she shouted over and over again. But there was no response. Miss Pepperdine dabbed his forehead with her damp handkerchief. He still did not stir. She thought of going to her parents' house to get help. Then she patted her cloth over his brow once more.

He moved. "I –I"

"Can you walk?" she shrieked.

"I think so." He stirred and with effort, wiggled his body into a sitting position.

"Thank the Lord. You're alright." Miss Pepperdine took a deep breath. "Cliff, if you can walk to my buckboard, I'll take you home.

"I think I can," he replied.

"Good," she said in relief.

* * *

Preacher Adam Miller whipped the reins, and his horses dug into the dirt as his buckboard moved forward toward Oakland, Nebraska. Dirt flew around him. He coughed and pulled up his large, red kerchief around his neck to pull the cloth over his mouth. Adam decided to visit this village, which was in close proximity to Tekamah, because that was the place where the voice contest would be held. Adam shook his head. *Could the boy get well by then?* He did not know; it was up to the Lord.

He passed small farms after small farms with cattle herds nibbling on the grasslands. Oakland looked a lot like Tekamah. However, this township had the added asset of Logan Creek, which provided a history of fresh water for many abundant years. Adam pulled up the beasts to the hitching post. He jumped down and wrapped the reins around the post. The sun beat down on his forehead. Sweat poured down his cheeks. He pulled off his kerchief and wiped the sweat off his brow.

The parson looked up at the majestic Lutheran church constructed of stone. It probably was at least three times the size of Cross Lutheran of Tekamah. The tall spiral cross gave it elegance and signaled to those lost to come inside and have peace in the Lord. Adam had to admit it was the perfect place to hold the competition. Each village in and around Burt County got to send their best singers. Tekamah had chosen Cliff. He was their best.

Pastor Adam stepped up the side stairs to enter the church. *Someone should be there to take our name for the competition.* He squeaked open the church door and stepped inside. There were a few people seated at a table to his left. Preacher examined the beautiful interior with its massive pipe organ taking center stage, and its long altar table covered with a white linen cloth.

Adam stared at the piano, which stood to the right of the organ. To the left was the parson lectern. *I wish our sanctuary could be as grand as theirs.* He shook his head. *God, I'm sorry for my sinful thought of envy. It isn't the place. It's getting people to Jesus.*

The minister approached the wooden table of seven men. He cleared his throat. "I'm – I'm here to place Tekamah's name in the voice competition. We've never participated before, but we've got a wonderful boy who is the greatest singer we've ever had."

The gray-haired man studied the pastor's face. "How old is the boy? Are you his father?"

"He's twelve years old but I'm not his father. His pa passed away a while ago. I'm his parson."

"Is the mother still alive? Does the family attend church regularly?"

"Yes, she is." The minister cleared his throat. "I – I . . ."

"The boy cannot compete unless his mother testifies to his Christian faith."

Pastor Adam shifted his feet back and forth. "He's a good, Christian boy. He is the eldest of the siblings, but his ma can't come here with the youngest being four years old, and all the rest are under twelve."

"I see. Could you vouch for the family?" The elderly man's countenance paled.

"I can for the boy."

"Not the family?"

"Don't know them well."

The old man whispered to the others at the table. After a few minutes passed, the interviewer raised his head. "You can sign up the boy, but we can't guarantee he'll be able to compete."

The minister gulped and added Cliff's name to the list. *Oh Lord, please let the boy sing. Even with him being sick, he's determined to win this.*

Chapter Eighteen

Erina took a seat near the church's front row in the hopes of seeing Cliff sing. He had missed two weeks so far. Scanning the sanctuary, she did not see him. *Oh Lord, please heal Cliff. He has so much talent and such a gift.* Erina searched the sanctuary once more. She did not see him.

Miss Pepperdine took her seat at the organ. The *organ* sat a few feet from the *piano*.

Not a good sign. For Erina knew Miss Pepperdine would have sat at the *piano* if Cliff were there.

The engagement of the parson to Erina swept the congregation like lilies bloom in spring. She raised her head toward the altar as Miss Nielsen scooted in beside Erina.

Nielsen turned to Erina. "Congratulations on your engagement. I was surprised to hear this news. I – I didn't think you two liked each other."

"Well, I think Preacher Adam was intrigued with me when we first met as classmates. But I didn't like him much since he played tricks on me."

"So he was one of those."

"What do you mean?" Erina asked.

"He was mischievous." Nielsen chuckled.

"Yes, he was but he's not like that now. He's a changed man since he found the Lord."

"I hope so. It's important that a minister stays upright, and your family was a good example of that. Your mother and father were pillars of the community, and I'm sure you will follow in their footsteps," Nielsen retorted.

Oh! My God. Erina gulped. Her face turned hot. *What if my family's secret is exposed? It will not only hurt my family's reputation and Lee's as well as Adam's.*

Miss Pepperdine ground out the first hymn, "Be Still, My Soul." That distracted Erina from thinking more about the ramifications of exposing the secret.

A young boy Erina never had seen before stepped down the aisle with a candlestick in hand to light the altar candles. His features looked a lot like Cliff's. *It couldn't be his brother, could it?* She fidgeted in her seat. *Cliff could not have sent him in his place, could he?* She hoped not, but she believed his siblings would do anything for their oldest brother.

* * *

Nielsen hastened toward the church door. *I've got to see if that young boy was Cliff's brother.* He looked so much like Cliff with his curly, carrot-red hair. She swung the entrance door open when the little boy snuck around her. "Are you Cliff's brother?" she shouted while he raced out the door. She stumbled. "Boy, you've got to have better manners than that! You almost caused me to fall."

"Sorry. Got to get home," the boy replied while he scurried toward the road.

Erina observed it all and rushed toward him. "How is Cliff? We're praying for him. "

The boy turned his face toward Erina. "Ain't doing so good. We'll see." He jerked his head to the road ahead.

Carol Nielsen maneuvered to Erina. "Is he Cliff's brother?"

"Don't know. Sure looks like Cliff," Erina replied.

The boy now had gotten ahead of them.

"What's your name," shouted Carol.

"Billy," the boy answered as he dug his feet into the earth and spurted toward the path that would take him to his Ma's.

"We've got to find out how Cliff is doing." Erina forced a smile.

"You're right. Parson Adam needs to make a visit." Carol Nielsen studied the betrothed, while the old parishioner tightened the ends of her hat as a sharp gust of wind whipped around them.

"I'll mention it to him," Erina responded as another whiff of wind tossed her hair in the air.

Carol stomped her feet. "Don't mention it to him. You *tell* him he needs to see that lad regardless of his mother's beliefs!"

* * *

Erina glanced at her brother's glowing face as the family gathered around her mother's dining-room table to celebrate her engagement to Pastor Adam. She poured the apple cider into the goblets.

Lee smiled and said the toast. "Mary and I lift our glasses to honor the engagement of you and Parson Adam. This is such a wonderful occasion. We're so happy for you both." Clanging the glasses together, each took sips of their drinks.

"This is such a grand time with our upcoming wedding and the birth of a niece or a nephew soon to be added to our family." Erina took another sip of the cider with Adam, Lee and Mary following. "How you feeling, Mary?" Erina asked with concern as her sister-in-law's face contorted in pain.

"I'm fine." Mary forced a smile.

"You sure you're fine?" Lee asked as he swooped over to his wife and clasped her hands.

Mary nodded.

Erina witnessed the love between them. "Soon that baby will be born, and you'll be fussing over the infant."

"And, you might not be long behind us," Lee replied with a chuckle in his voice while he loosed his grip on Mary's hand.

"I hadn't thought of that. You could be right," she said as she glanced over at Adam.

"You can have the girl and I'll have the boy." Adam's lips had parted into a large grin. He laughed.

"Over my dead body," Lee responded with a twinkle in his eye.

Erina stood up and stepped into the kitchen. Adam followed her. She took her hand masher and mashed the potatoes and added butter and milk. "You take the mashed potatoes, and I'll bring in the gravy and the green beans."

He winked at her. "What about the chicken?"

"Of course." She giggled. "It's all on the pink and rose china platter. We can't forget that."

Adam set the chicken and potatoes on the table.

Erina brought in the beans and gravy. "Lee, would you say grace?"

Lee nodded. "May the Lord bless this food as we celebrate the engagement of my sister to Parson Adam."

Erina laughed. "That's an awfully short blessing, Lee."

"I know but the smell of that fried chicken quickened my desire to dig into the food." He laughed.

Adam placed a breast and a leg on his plate then he passed the chicken platter to his left.

When the platter got to Erina, she took a wing then raised her head to the group. "It's good to have all of you together. I just hope Cliff is well enough to compete in the competition this Saturday."

Chapter Nineteen

Billy snuck into his brother's bedroom, carrying a metal cup of warm water, which contained one teaspoon of apple-cider vinegar and a teaspoon of raw honey. He put the object on the bedside table before he shook Cliff. "Wake up! Me got you something that will make you well."

Cliff's eyes opened. However, a minute later he fell asleep.

"Don't go back to sleep," protested Cliff's younger brother. "You got to drink this. It will make you better." Billy set the drink down then he pushed at Cliff's shoulders. "Open your eyes!"

Cliff's eyes spun open. He looked down at his smaller brother. "I'm going to die. Can't you see how sick I am? Leave me alone. It's useless."

"No, it ain't. Only God makes that decision, and you can beat it with this!" Billy responded while he reached for the metal cup.

"I don't believe that," Cliff muttered.

"Then you don't love the Lord like you said. Otherwise you would swallow this and see if it cures you."

Cliff forced his eyes open. "Who told you this could work?"

"Some church members said they knew people who have used this, and they got well."

"But I've got scarlet fever, and it has killed many."

"You don't know that."

"But-but people say I have it."

"Yes, and they could be wrong." Billy tightened his grip on the mug. "Let's see what happens. It's only vinegar and honey. Won't harm you either way." Billy forced the cup into Cliff's hands. "Drink! Drink!" the younger brother barked.

Cliff examined the potion in front of him. He lifted it up to his lips before he lowered it to its original place. "I just don't know," he wheezed.

"You drink or I'll tell Ma about you believing in Christ."

"Don't do that. It will break her heart."

"Then swallow this," Billy demanded.

Cliff's hands shook as he drew the drink to his lips and drank the liquid. "I don't think it's going to make me better."

"We'll see," Billy whispered as he heard footsteps approach. He grabbed the empty metal mug and placed it in one of his trouser pockets.

Ma swung the door open and rushed into the room. "Billy, I told you to stay away from your brother. "He's sick and I don't want you getting it. Get out of here, right now," she shouted.

Billy lowered his head and exited the room. He took a deep breath and scooted around her. Once outside the room, he pulled the object out of his pocket, wiped the cup with a flour cloth before he returned the metal mug to the cabinet.

* * *

Doctor Ben Moore knocked on the dilapidated door of the Gregorys. He waited several minutes then knocked again. Through the holes in the rickety front door, he witnessed a stampede of children rushing around the room. "You young'uns stop it. Someone is at the door," a mature woman's voice yelled. Footsteps creaked on the wooden floor. She squeaked the door open.

"Yes?" she asked.

Dr. Moore cleared his throat. "I'm here to look in on your sick boy."

"What you doing here? Who brought you? We don't have money to pay you. Understand?" Mrs. Gregory asked.

"I do. There's no charge for my visit. A wealthy church-going member paid for me to visit your oldest boy."

"I don't cotton to religious people. We've learned to make our own way without the Christ. He's brought me enough grief."

"I understand. I'm not here to bring you to Jesus, but I am here to see how your eldest is fairing." He swallowed hard, knowing that was the truth, but he hoped his visit would also open her heart to the Lord, where true love stems.

Using the sleeve of her soiled dress, she wiped her eyes. She opened the door wide. "Come on in. Got lots of children so lots of dirt."

The doctor nodded.

She stepped toward Cliff's room. "It ain't going to be pretty. I put him in my room to keep the others from catching it."

"How's he doing?" the doctor asked while they strode toward the room.

"Don't know. Ain't checked on him lately." She squeaked the door open and stared at Cliff sitting up in bed. "What you doing up?"

"I feel better," Cliff responded as he scooted his body further toward the headboard. "Who's he?" the boy asked his mother.

"He's a doctor," she replied. "What did you say your name was?" Ma turned to him.

"I'm Doctor Ben Moore."

"You from around here?" Cliff asked.

"Yup. Live in the small town up the road." He spread open his leather Gladstone bag, which contained a thermometer, a stethoscope, a tongue depressor, a hammer and catgut for bandaging.

"Your complexion looks pretty good," he said while he pulled out the thermometer from his bag. "Just seeing if you have a fever. This instrument will tell me that, but you're only lightly flushed and that's good." He shook the thermometer. "Open your mouth wide."

The boy did as the doctor ordered.

Then the doctor placed the instrument inside his mouth. He opened his pocket watch. "Let's play a game while we wait. I'm going to ask you a few questions.

Cliff nodded.

"Is your throat sore?"

"It was but not now," Cliff replied.

The doctor grinned. "How about headaches?"

"Had one yesterday but it's gone, also," the boy said.

"How's your stomach?" he asked as he looked at his pocket watch.

"A little queasy the last few days, but I'm fine today."

"Well, this is all wonderful. Now open your mouth." He pulled the thermometer out of Cliff's mouth and examined the large, fat instrument.

The boy chuckled. "I just want to get out of this bed. I feel better, and I don't think God's calling me."

Doctor Moore glanced at the thermometer. "Well, I've got a lot of great news for you. "Your temperature is normal, and you don't have scarlet fever. I think you had strep throat. In some ways, they can have the same symptoms." He grinned. "Now you can sing in that contest. I've heard your voice is as sweet to listen to as honey."

Cliff pulled the blanket off of him. He gave a soft laugh. "Honey and apple-cider vinegar is what Billy made me take."

"What a great combination." The corners of the doctor's face curved up into a smile.

"Well, I wouldn't call it great tasting. Sour and honey aren't the best, but I'll take it." Cliff jumped down off of the bed.

"Now, don't you overdo," the doctor said in a stern voice. "I'll tell your ma you are no longer sick, but you watch yourself." He followed the boy out the bedroom door. *Pastor Adam and the congregation are going to be relieved. Thank God I came here and can give them the good news.*

* * *

"Climb in, Cliff. We're ready to go. Don't be nervous. You'll do fine." Preacher Adam turned his head to the doctor. "You ready to testify on Cliff's behalf?"

"I'm ready and am happy to do this," Doctor Moore stated. He grinned at Cliff as the boy scooted next to the doctor on the buckboard seat.

Preacher Adam flapped the reins of the beasts while they headed to Oakland. The buckboard bounced while the horses stirred up dust as their hoofs dug into the dirt.

Some of the particles entered into Cliff's lungs; he coughed.

The doctor pulled the kerchief, which hung around his neck, off of him then presented it to Cliff. "The last thing we need is for this dust to affect your voice. You take it and pull it up over your mouth when needed. We're all praying for you."

"Thank you," retorted Cliff while he wrapped the large, red kerchief around his own neck to draw up over his mouth when needed.

The steeds swerved past the cattle grazing. The light spring breeze made everything perfect. Cliff shifted his head to the men. "I hope you and Doctor Moore are allowed to testify to my Christian faith.

"Don't lose faith. God is with you," replied the parson.

Doctor Moore nodded.

The steeds' hoofs thundered on the brick streets. Soon Pastor Adam slowed the steeds to a halt. He jumped down then wrapped the reins around the hitching post. The doctor and Cliff stood in front of the preacher. The parson turned to them. "Let's say a prayer. May the Lord be with us today, and may Cliff do well in the competition. Amen."

* * *

Cliff gulped, hoping he could sing in the competition. With the preacher and doctor's testimonies, he believed his chances would improve, but there was no guarantee. He thought of all that happened in the past weeks from the competition's standards of only being able to compete if his family went to church, and he hoped the illness had not damaged his ability to do his best.

Although his younger brother, Billy, found the Lord, the rest of the family had not. His mother's heart still hardened.

Cliff marched down the sanctuary aisle, hoping everything would go well as he entered the room. He swallowed the lump in his throat as he approached the long table of seven men. Cliff stood in front of them. "I'm – I'm," he gulped, "I'm here to participate in the contest."

The older gray-headed man studied him from head to toe. "Your face is white. You sure you're up to this?" the man bellowed out.

Cliff nodded.

The man stroked his beard while he whispered to the man next to him. Soon the topic reached the rest of those at the table. He took a deep breath. "You sure look mighty pale."

The doctor and pastor Adam reached the table. "The boy is with us," stated the parson. "With me is the doctor who looked in on him, while he was under the weather."

"I'm Doctor Moore. I examined the boy three days ago and determined him well enough to compete in this event."

The gray-haired man lifted his countenance to the physician. "Well, you know a lot more about health and such than what I know." He turned to the rest of those at the table. Each nodded in agreement. The elderly man lifted his head to Cliff. "I guess you are in fine shape. What's your name, boy?"

"Cliff Gregory," the boy replied.

The older man scratched his forehead. "And you're from where?"

"Tekamah."

"Tekamah." The man's brow furrowed. "You're the one we haven't given our final blessing. Your Pa's dead, correct?"

Cliff nodded.

"You're Ma?

"She had five young'uns. I'm – I'm the eldest," Cliff stammered.

"I see. Are you regular churchgoers?"

"I am," he gulped, "and my brother Billy also goes to services."

The old man stroked his beard once more. He stared at the boy. "Every participant must have the blessing of the church. We haven't given ours since your Ma cannot vouch for the family's Christian faith."

"Ma never missed a church service until –" the boy's voice trailed off. Then he turned his head from the bearded questioner. A tear dripped down the boy's cheek. He took a deep breath, faced the man and blurted out his answer. "She lost my pa in a carriage roadside accident returning from church with my youngest sister, Doria." Cliff swayed from one foot to another. "From there on, she blamed God and has not returned to church." The boy's lips quivered. "I'm sorry but I believe."

* * *

Parson Adam stretched out his arm and clasped the boy's hand. "I'm sure your ma went through a terrible time after your pa passed. I wasn't the pastor then, so I did not know what happened. I hope the money I gave you has helped your family."

Cliff nodded. "It's helped a lot."

"Good," the preacher responded.

Doctor Moore grasped Cliff's wrist. "We understand. Don't fret." The doctor lifted his countenance to the questioner. "Please let the boy sing. You'll find pleasure in listening to his voice. He's a good Christian boy."

The elderly man gazed at the other men around the table. They nodded. "We're in agreement. You're accepted in the competition."

"I'm so grateful. Thank you." Cliff smiled, and the pastor and doctor released their grip on the boy.

"Sit over there," stated the older gentlemen, "and await your turn. When we call your city or town, then you'll come forward. State the name of the tune you're to sing, and the pianist will play it. The audience's applause will determine the winner."

Cliff nodded and took a seat.

Doctor Moore sat to the boy's right and Preacher Adam to the boy's left. The parson leaned to Cliff and whispered, "Take a deep breath and relax. The Lord is with you."

Chapter Twenty

Cliff observed the contest.

"The loudest clapping at each end of the performances determines the winner," stated the master of ceremony. He paused then shouted, "West Point."

A young, pretty, blonde girl around the age of ten years old, who wore an ivory pinafore and a printed blouse underneath, stepped toward the pianist before she placed her hymnal on the wooden musical stand then the girl turned to the hymn she planned to sing.

The woman placed her hands on the keys and began playing.

The contestant swayed back and forth as she sang "I am Jesus' little lamb, Ever glad at heart I am; For my Shepherd gently guides me, Knows my need, and well provides me, Loves me every day the same, Even calls me by my name . . ."

Rounds of clapping ensued, including the preacher, doctor and Cliff as she exited the stage.

"What a cutie," whispered Parson Adam to Cliff.

Cliff nodded.

The master of ceremony strode toward the long altar table then paused and yelled, "Arlington."

An eight-year-old boy stepped to the piano and whispered to the pianist. He wore a hat, knickers and a suit coat. He placed his hymnal on the stand then nodded to the pianist. "While Shepherds Watched Their Flocks by Night, All seated on the ground, . . ."

Cliff grinned and spoke to the doctor in a quiet voice, "That's a Christmas hymn."

"I know," Doctor Moore muttered in response. "I don't know if the audience is in the mood for that this time of year." He hesitated then a splatter of clapping emerged. "See, people didn't like it."

One after another contestant approached the piano and belted out their songs. Cliff wiggled in his seat. The longer the boy sat there the more anxious he became. He wiped his brow with the doctor's kerchief. His knee bobbed up and down.

Parson Adam leaned toward the boy beside him. "Relax," muttered the preacher.

"How do I do that?" Cliff asked.

"Take deep breaths and pray."

Cliff gulped and prayed.

Then the master of ceremony spoke, "Tekamah."

As Cliff approached the piano, he realized he left his song sheet in his pew seat. Cliff panicked. He glanced up at the pianist and placed his arms on his hips in disgust. His face grew hot. Stepping to her, he whispered the tune he wanted.

She searched her hymnal and did not find the song. The pianist shrugged.

The master of ceremony approached Cliff and spoke out loud: "We'll give you five minutes to find your song or we'll move on." The man pulled out his pocket watch and studied it.

Cliff rocked from one foot to the other.

The master of ceremony began to speak.

It's now or ever. He took a deep breath, and his deep bass voice rolled out without the accompaniment. "Amazing grace! How sweet the sound, That saved a wretch like me! I once was lost, but now am found, Was blind, but now I see . . ." T. hen he finished with these words: "We've no less days to sing God's praise, Than when we first begun."

The room exploded with the audience standing and clapping. Hoots and hollers joined the applause as Cliff left the stage to return to his seat.

* * *

The master of ceremony returned. "We will have a fifteen-minute intermission before the winner is announced."

Cliff yawned. "I'm sorry but sitting here makes you sleepy," he said to his companions before he stood up to stretch his legs. Pastor Adam and the doctor joined him.

"There were a lot of good singers," the boy said.

The reverend turned to Doctor Moore. "Yes, but in my judgment yours was the best."

"I agree," chimed in the doctor.

"Well, no matter. It's an honor."

The master of ceremony stood in front of the altar. "I want to thank all who participated in this annual event. We are grateful for the wonderful talent we have here. It is unanimous that the winner this year is Cliff Gregory of Tekamah. Come up here and receive your award."

As Cliff sprinted to stand beside the master of ceremony, rounds of clapping ensured.

"Your voice is deep and soothing, and we are honored to present you the monetary award, but in addition, our Pastor Quinn has donated a family Bible. This Bible includes pages of Jewish history, places to enter marriages and other occasions as well as those who have passed on, thus this Book will guide you throughout your life. Please lift up this Bible so all can see the value of having such a gift."

Cliff smiled before he showed the black-leather, heavy Bible with the letters, Holy Bible in gold, to the audience. Then he opened the Bible and showed the audience the first page where Cliff's name appeared. "Thank you so much Reverend Thomas Quinn. I – I don't have a Bible of my own," Cliff stammered. He pressed the large Bible to his chest. He stood there a moment. His lips trembled with gratitude as he spoke. "I'm so appreciative of these gifts. I couldn't have received a better present than this Bible for its impact on my life will last forever."

The crowd burst in another round of applause.

"This ends our closing ceremony. Don't forget our competition next year, so get your voices ready. He smiled before he turned to Cliff.

With a grin as wide as the Mississippi River, Cliff strode off the stage with his new Bible and the fifty-dollar cash reward inserted inside one of the Bible's pages for safekeeping.

* * *

"You've got to sing that hymn at church. Just like you sang it so well today," muttered the preacher while he unwound the reins from the hitching post. The steeds neighed.

"I don't know," replied skeptical Cliff. "Ma might hear about it and that will cause problems." The boy sat on the hard, wooden buckboard seat.

The doctor followed and sat beside Cliff.

The preacher snapped the reins and the horses moved forward. A cool breeze brushed against them while Adam guided the horses toward Tekamah. Preacher Adam grinned while an idea fetched through his brain. He turned to the boy. "You know that Erina has agreed to marry me."

Cliff nodded with a puzzled look.

"We decided to marry at the end of October, and yet we failed to ask you to sing at our wedding." Adam gulped. "So would you?"

A long silence followed. Cliff cleared his throat, "It would be a pleasure, of course. Do you have a song in mind?"

Adam's brow creased as his mind searched for appropriate tunes to fit the occasion. The steeds clomped on the brick pavement until they left Oakland then the beasts stirred up the dust. The pastor swallowed some of the dirt before he returned his response to Cliff. "What about 'Blest Be the Tie That Binds'? The song could come right before our vows.

Doctor Moore chimed in. "That sounds grand." He turned to Cliff. "What do you think?"

"Sounds good, but I'll need time to practice," Cliff replied in a nervous tone.

"That's fine," retorted Adam, "we'll pay you for the singing. The date is Saturday, October seventeenth. Pastor Quinn will conduct the ceremony."

"I am honored and happy to do the singing, Cliff replied, his voice now strong then his lips spread into a large grin.

"We are proud of you. I wish your mother could join in the celebration, " Adam added, while he steered the horses homeward. He glanced at Cliff whose face turned crimson.

* * *

Erina opened the door to her brother and sister-in-law. "I'm ready," she said, her

voice near a whisper. She turned to Mary. "What— what do you think?" Erina twirled around in her long white laced wedding dress.

"Oh, Erina, you did such a grand job. You look so beautiful, and I love the laced- ruffled bodice and the necklace of pearls accenting your high-neck collar. It's just lovely."

"Thank you. I've been working on this dress ever since Parson Adam asked me to marry him, and the pearls were our mother's." Erina took a deep breath as she draped her mother's velvet beaded and feathered trimmed cape around her. Her gaze went to her brother, Lee.

"You make the Higgins proud," he said, "and you look beautiful with ma's cape over your shoulders."

"I hope so. I wish Ma were here." Then she thought of the family's secret. She really shouldn't marry, but she loved that exasperating Adam from his mischievous years to his strength in the Lord and sweet kisses. Tears dripped down Erina's cheeks. She snuffed them out with her embroidered handkerchief. "I'm nervous but ready to go."

"Of course, you're anxious. If you weren't, I'd think something was wrong with you," stated Mary as she tightened her wrap around her. Lee ushered his wife onto the buckboard seat.

"How you feeling, Mary?" asked Erina while she scooted onto the seat next to her brother's wife.

"Oh, I'm feeling better, and the child inside me is growing. I feel like I've got a large pumpkin sitting on my stomach," Mary replied, her voice light and airy.

Erina laughed as Lee snapped the reins. The burnt orange, rustic red and chocolate-brown leaves graced the trees while others spread across the earth. The steeds crunched over the fallen leaves and moved forward toward the downward plunge to the church.

Chapter Twenty-One

Miss Pepperdine smiled down at her parents, Cliff, Lee and preacher Adam, who stood waiting for the rest of the bridal party, as the organist put her hands on the keys and began playing, "I am Jesus' Little Lamb."

It was then that little Gerdie Richmonds, who lived down the hill from Parson Adam, swayed down the aisle, wearing a pale-yellow bonnet, which matched her cotton dress trimmed with lace at the bottom of her long sleeves and around her collar. Gerdie's small grin lit up the sanctuary while she carried a basket of autumn leaves and spread them on the church's wooden planks as she strode down the aisle then stood to the left of the church's altar.

The organist played, "Here Comes the Bride."

The congregation turned to observe the bride. Erina strode down the aisle. Her lace gown swirled around her ankles while she marched toward her husband to be. The pearls decorated around her high-neck collar danced in the autumn light through the church windows. She stopped in front of Reverend Thomas Quinn, the preacher from Oakland.

The smiling parson, whose long hair touched his shoulders, wore a frock coat and white cravat tucked inside his black waistcoat. The pastor nodded to the couple once they stood in front of him and directed his attention to Adam. "Wilt thou have this Woman to be thy wedded wife? Wilt thou love her, comfort her, honor and keep her in sickness and in health . . . so long as ye both shall live?"

"I will," replied Adam. He glanced over at his adoring wife to be.

The Oakland preacher continued and turned to Erina. "Wilt thou have this Man to be thy wedded husband to live together after God's ordinance in the holy estate of Matrimony? Wilt thou obey him and serve him, love, honor and keep him in sickness and in health, keep thee only unto him, so long as ye both shall live?"

"I will," she replied in a meek voice.

"Who giveth this woman to be married to this man?" He searched the room until his eyes settled on her brother, Lee.

"I do." Then Lee returned to his seat beside his wife.

Cliff pulled the wedding band from his little finger and presented it to Parson Quinn.

The preacher spoke, "With this ring, I thee wed, and with all my worldly goods, I thee endow. In the name of the Father, and of the Son, and of the Holy Ghost. Amen." He lifted up a prayer and placed the couple's right hands together. "Those whom God hath joined together let no man put asunder." Then the parson said a blessing. "God the Father, bless, preserve, and keep you . . . that ye may so live together . . . have life everlasting. Amen." He nodded to Cliff.

Miss Pepperdine returned her hands to the keys and began playing the tune, " Blest Be the Tie That Binds."

Cliff opened his lips wide, and his deep voice rang out the hymn. "Blest be the tie that binds, Our hearts in Christian love; The fellowship of kindred minds, Is like to that above. ..."

Eyes misty, Erina turned to her husband. He smiled at her while they stepped down the aisle as one.

After the ceremony, Miss Pepperdine strode to Cliff. Her lips quivered as she spoke, "You did a grand job. This wedding will be remembered for a long time because of your singing."

* * *

Cliff stood outside as the wedding guests shook his hand to congratulate him for the stirring rendition of "Blest Be the Tie That Binds."

The Oakland parson approached Cliff. "Your voice is one in a million. It's deep yet it's moving. I'm so proud of you." He stuck out his arm to shake Cliff's hand. "You will go far as long as you follow the Lord."

"Thank you and I hope I will never fail Him." The boy shook the pastor's hand.

"Remember you are human and you'll make mistakes. Just ask the Lord to forgive you because no one is perfect, son." Preacher Quinn stepped to Cliff's right while one after another approached the boy to express their appreciations.

* * *

Pastor Adam and Erina strode to Cliff. Lee and Mary stood beside them. Preacher Adam spoke first. "You did an awesome job. We're proud of you." He gave Cliff a gentle slap on his back.

Erina grinned. "You made our wedding special." Then she laughed. "I guess all are special, aren't they? But your voice made it extra exceptional." She turned to Pastor

Quinn. "Thank you for doing the honors. We sure couldn't have Adam here do his own vows."

Quinn laughed. He studied her from the bottom of her dress to the top of her head. "You look exactly like a woman I knew back in New York. She was a beautiful lady. Her last name was Higgins like yours. Did you ever live back East?"

"I was a little girl when we left New York. I didn't know I looked liked my ma." Erina clamped her lips together before she opened her mouth. She coughed. "Mother passed away a few months back."

"Oh, I'm sorry." He touched his forehead. "There was some kind of scandal if my memory is correct. Is that why your family left?"

"Yes." She gulped. Erina took a deep breath. She knew she could not lie in church. So instead, teardrops fell down her cheeks. Erina turned to her brother and her sister-in-law. "Mother had an affair with a New York tycoon. The scandal was unbearable. That's why we left." Her voice broke.

Adam wrapped his arms around her. He held her for a long time as droplets dripped down her cheeks.

Preacher Quinn's face turned red. "I'm sorry. I didn't mean to cause problems. Curiosity killed the cat," he mumbled while he stepped toward his horse-drawn carriage.

"I've made our happy event a sad one. Hope you don't hate me," she squeaked to Adam.

"Never. I love you, and remember the Lord ordained our union." Adam chuckled. Erina gave a soft laugh. Shaking, she gazed at her brother and sister-in-law. They glared at them.

* * *

Adam wrapped Erina's treasured cape of her mother's over his wife's shoulders. Then he guided her to their buckboard before he helped her onto the seat. "It's going to be fine, Erina; God is with us."

"I hope so," she mumbled.

"He is. We'll get through this," he replied while he boarded the wagon.

"I shouldn't have married you. Look at what I have caused," she cried, as she tied the bonnet ribbons underneath her chin while the buckboard bounced toward home.

"You've caused nothing. It wasn't *your* sin but *your mother's* that created this scandal." Adam paused then took a deep breath and squeezed her left hand. "Don't worry. Have faith, sweetheart. Have faith," he reiterated.

Adam flapped the reins to speed up the horses. The cool air swirled around them. The horses crunched over the leaves as they headed to Erina's house. He gulped, knowing as a preacher of the Word, some of the members would leave the church or try to replace him with another. However, he could not worry Erina. The parson took a deep breath. He turned to Erina and cocked a grin. "You ready for an array of kisses?"

"As ready as I'll ever be," she said with a laugh. Erina turned her face from him and wrapped the cape tighter around her.

"Good, for my lips are prepared," he said with a chuckle while the buckboard rattled into the Erina's barn. He jumped down from the carriage and went over to his wife. He gave her a suspicious smile while he aided her from the buckboard. He lifted her up into his arms and strode toward the house.

"What you doing?" she cried.

"Why, I'm doing what any husband would do!"

"What's that?" she asked, her face and hands cool from the autumn air.

His eyes twinkled. "Why, I'm – I'm doing my duty."

"What duty? You're baffling me."

He rushed her to the front door, pushed it open and carried her over the threshold. He gingerly placed her on the parlor floor.

She giggled. "You didn't have to do that."

"Yes, I did," he responded. Then he smothered her with sweet kisses from the top of her head to her nose and mouth. Once done, he studied her surprised countenance and laughed. "Now, I've fulfilled my *threshold* duties."

Chapter Twenty-Two

Erina could not stop the tears from flowing down her cheeks. She tried to brush them aside using her flour dish towel, but the tears still fell as she bent down to crack the eggs into the fry pan's grease.

Adam stepped into the kitchen and cocked a smile. "Well, hello, my sweetheart."

Avoiding his gaze, she studied the eggs in the pan before she placed them on their plates.

He came closer to her and planted two kisses on her forehead. "Don't worry. God is with us.

"But–but, it's all my fault."

"No, it's not. Your mother sinned, not you or the rest of your family."

She attempted to go around him to put the pink-and-rose plates on the dining-room table.

Instead, he took the dishes away from her and placed them on the now cold stove.

"The eggs are going to get cold," she exclaimed while she tried to reach the plates.

"No way!" he chuckled while he wrapped his arms around her. "I can eat eggs cold, and besides there are better things to do like caressing lips." He brought her to him and kissed her from the tip of her forehead to the bottom of her chin. Adam finally released her.

Out of breath, she lifted her head to him. "What am I going to do with you?"

"Love me and do not be afraid says the Bible 365 times," he retorted with a wry smile.

Exasperated, she shook her head and laughed.

* * *

Cliff strode to his mother's house. Billy stepped beside him.

He lifted his head to his elder brother. "That was one bewitching ceremony."

"Bewitching!" Cliff chuckled, while he strode around the autumn leaves and dying grasses. "I just hope Ma ain't mad at us.

"She'd better not be. Billy chuckled. "I'll have to tell her you roped me into this."

Cliff gulped while he thought about his little brother's remark. *Would Billy betray him?* He needed his support in case his mother did hear about his singing. He cleared his throat and breathed in the cool air. "You wouldn't do that to your older brother, would you?

Billy shook his head, no.

That wasn't reassuring. His mother's tiny board-and-batten structure stood in front of them. Cliff opened the door with his brother following.

Mother stood in front of them. "What you two up to? You've been gone all afternoon, and I needed someone to help with the young'uns."

Billy chimed in, "We've been . . ."

"Been fishing," Cliff lied as his cheeks became hot.

"You're telling tales. I can see it on your faces. I'll get to the bottom of this as soon as I dish out the porridge," she said while scooping out the grains into the bowls.

"Porridge, again," said Billy while he shifted his feet from one to the other.

"Yes, and that's the way it is until I remarry," their mother retorted in a shaky voice.

"But, I could make money . . ." Cliff stopped himself from finishing the rest of his sentence.

"How?" Ma stared at her eldest son. "You not making sense."

"Singing," chimed in Billy.

Cliff cleared his throat. "Yes, he's right."

"You both got a touch of madness." Ma slammed the bowls on the table. "Eat it before it gets cold."

Cliff gulped. He wanted to share his singing success with his ma, but instead, he grabbed a bowl and sat down to eat.

* * *

Billy pulled out a chair and sat beside his elder brother. He turned to Cliff. "Why don't you tell Ma then we could quit eating porridge? I'm sick of it.' He took a bite and spit it out. "Ma!" he yelled.

She turned her attention to Billy.

"Cliff sings at church and he won a voice contest."

"What?" Her brow creased.

Cliff's lips trembled. "I'm sorry," he mumbled.

She rushed over to Cliff. "I thought you were helping the minister, not joining in on their church service. Tell me the truth."

"Billy – Billy, is giving you the truth," Cliff responded, his eyes downcast. "Jesus is my Savior."

"Oh no, I can't believe one of my own found the Lord. You know I hate that after what happened to Pa." Ma glared at her oldest son. "You and Billy are forbidden to attend church. From now on, you'll stay here. I won't tolerate it!"

"Then I won't have the extra money I get for helping the parson during service," chimed in Cliff.

"The preacher gives me money at times as well," added Billy.

Ma's countenance turned crimson. She took several deep breaths. "I guess you'll have to continue since we need the money. However, no more singing during church. Do you hear me?"

Cliff nodded.

Ma turned her face from them for a few minutes before she readdressed them. "I won't hear any more of this, for I've got to protect my other children."

"Ma, you once loved . . ." Cliff could not finish his sentence. He lifted a silent prayer to the Almighty.

Billy's lips quivered, knowing he made two enemies today – Cliff and his mother. Billy pushed himself closer to the table and forced the porridge down his throat.

* * *

Adam hitched up the steeds. Erina scooted onto the buckboard seat. Tears streaked down her cheeks. He gulped as the rig exited the barn. This Sunday was like no other. The whole community knew about Erina's family secret, and Cliff was no longer able to grace the church with his heavenly voice. *Lord, I know you are with me. Help us to weather this storm.*

He gulped while he thought of Erina's brother and sister-in-law. They, too, kept their distance. Erina had not seen or talked to them since the wedding, which was a month ago. Last Sunday, there was a spattering of attendance from Miss Pepperdine and her family to Lucas Pierce, his wife and their four boys; Carol Nielsen, Doctor Moore; and Adam's parents. Adam clamped his lips together. *What awaited him today?*

The buckboard rattled as Adam guided the horse-drawn carriage down the small hill. The cool air brushed against them. Adam prayed, "Lord, I ask that no rain falls and more people show up." He steered the animals onto the church grounds and pulled the rig up to the hitching post. Adam jumped down and tied up the steeds. He strode to Erina and stretched out his cold hand to assist her.

She stumbled and fell into his arms. He tightened his grip before releasing her. *Oh no, here comes busybody Carol Nielsen. That's all I need.*

Carol stood in front of them. She lifted her head to them and curled up her nose. "Like daughter like mother," she spat. "You ought to know better than being intimate in front of people."

"We weren't, Adam said. "Erina fell out of the carriage and ended up in my arms."

"I bet!" Carol laughed then she headed for the sanctuary.

Shaking, Erina stood beside her husband. Tears dripped down her cheeks. "Look what I have caused. I'm – I'm so very sorry."

He tightened his cold-hand grip on Erina's hand as they stepped to the church. Once inside, he released his hand from hers. She strode toward the sanctuary while Adam progressed to his office to put on his robe before he entered the church's chancel area.

Adam's throat tightened while he scanned the sanctuary in front of him. He smiled down at his doctor friend before he glanced at Carol Nielsen, Lucas Pierce, without his wife and family, and Miss Pepperdine, the organist, and her parents. Taking a deep breath, his gaze settled on his wife then he forced a smile. He was determined to not let Erina know the devastating situation he faced. The board would seek his resignation if low attendance proceeded as it was now.

Adam looked at the congrats and said, "Thank you for coming. God bless you one and all." The service continued until it was time for the hymn to be sung after leading the congregation in reciting the Lord's Prayer.

Parson Adam swallowed the lump in his throat. Eyes downcast, he heard a rush of footsteps and opened his eyes to see Cliff, Billy and their mother and the rest of the family all sitting in the front pew next to Erina. *What is this about?* Reverend Adam glanced at Miss Pepperdine to play the hymn.

With a large grin, Miss Pepperdine placed her fingers on the keys. As she did that, Cliff raced up the steps and stood beside the organist.

His rich bass voice rang out: "The King of Love my Shepherd is, Whose goodness failed never; I nothing lack if I am His, And He is mine forever."

Then one family member after another stepped inside with Reverend Thomas Quinn following. Each took a seat as Cliff finished the tune with these words: "In death's dark vale I fear no ill, With thee, dear Lord, beside me, Thy rod and staff my comfort still, Thy cross before to guide me."

Baffled, Pastor Adam gulped. He did not know what to make of it. He recited the benediction and then marched down the aisle to greet those in attendance. Erina stood outside beside him. The sweet-morning sun provided them warmth in the autumn air.

Adam raised his arm to shake Cliff's hand. "I'm so happy you returned." The preacher's voice broke a second. "We missed you."

"Happy to be back. Ma and the family came, too," Cliff responded,

"I saw that, and I thank the Man Upstairs for all of it." The minister shook each hand. He stopped a second and whispered to Reverend Thomas Quinn, "Please join us for breakfast this morning. I'm anxious to find out how Cliff and his family showed up today."

Chapter Twenty-Three

Erina set the table for a late morning breakfast. She turned to Reverend Thomas Quinn as he entered the dining room. "Have a seat. Everything is ready." She poured the coffee into the pink-and-rose cups.

"Thank you for inviting me. You have a nice home," Quinn replied while he scanned the dining room.

"It isn't much. But my parents were happy here. Both are gone now." Erina choked.

" I see that still grieves you," Quinn responded. "I know all about that since l lost my wife last year. She passed away after giving birth to our second son."

"So sorry," chimed in Parson Adam. "Life sure brings sorrows, but joy comes in the morning. " He paused a moment then asked, "Would you say grace, Reverend Quinn?

Minister Quinn nodded and clasped his hands together. "We come to you, Lord, with Your gratefulness that provides each day with strength to persevere. God bless this food. Amen."

"Thank you," responded Erina in a low voice as she wiped the dripping tears with her fingertips.

Quinn took a biscuit, two fried eggs and three pieces of bacon from the gold-edged platter with violet flowers before passing it to his left. "Thanks for inviting me to breakfast," Quinn said. He buttered his biscuit, cut into one of the eggs and chewed into one piece of the tantalizing bacon. "Mighty good," he said after he finished the bacon.

Erina turned to her brother and his wife. "There's plenty of food, so don't be afraid that I'll run out."

"I won't." Lee laughed. "However, I must confess I'm ashamed of not standing up for my sister. I – I am sorry."

"Don't be," she replied, "for the Lord is good, and He enabled us to survive this storm."

Adam could no longer be still. He turned to Reverend Quinn. "How did you get Cliff's family to show up? I've got to know," he rushed out the words.

Quinn grabbed his fork and finished eating his second egg. Then he lifted his face toward Adam. "I kept thinking about Cliff and his deep bass voice. He has such talent."

"I liked the boy." He sipped his coffee then turned to Erina. "There's no reason the congregation should shun you when you were *not* the one who sinned. It was your mother's fault, not yours, and I know she suffered greatly from having to live a common man's life instead of the wealth she had in New York. However, sin has consequences.

"Word continued to trickle to Oakland, and I heard about how the congregation had turned against you, Parson Adam. That's when I decided I had to visit Cliff's house and see if I could talk to his ma. I knew if that family returned to church, others would follow. I asked the Lord for me to say the right words.

"Cliff's ma met me at the door of her house. The children were playing outside in the fall air, thus I could reveal things without them hearing our conversation. The shack and her soiled dress told me all I needed to know. She was hurting after losing her husband like I was after my wife passed away.

"We had that in common. Underneath the dirt and her circumstances, I saw the glimmer of a pretty woman who needed love. That's when I revealed how the Lord healed my heart, and how I became closer to Him after my wife's death.

"Cliff's ma cried. I hugged her as she let go of her grief. We connected. When I asked her and the children to meet me at the Lutheran church this Sunday, she agreed." He buttered the other half of his biscuit. His face paled. "She's a good woman. We agreed we would share our grief together, and let the Lord heal our hurts."

"Oh, thank you for taking the time to talk to her. It's wonderful that she has the Lord in her life once more." Then Adam turned to his wife. "See, I told you the Lord would work this out."

Erina pushed her chair back and stood up before she rushed to her husband and gave him a kiss on his forehead and a big hug. "You were so right. God saw us through this." Tears of joy flowed down her cheeks. "With Him by our side, we'll survive whatever hardships come our way."

Then Erina turned to her sister-in-law, Mary, who held her infant son in her arms. "Glorious," Erina shouted and turned her attention to her husband. "We've got the best gift from Heaven, our new nephew." The baby cried. Erina stepped to Mary and beamed at the child in Mary's lap. *The Lord is good. He's so very good.*

* * *

Reverend Thomas Quinn glanced at his beautiful bride, Helen Gregory. He could not believe how nervous he was. For after all, he had married many couples. *But those were members of his church, not my own wedding.* He took a deep breath while he waited for the ceremony to proceed.

Parson Adam Miller officiated. He grinned as he lowered his head to them. "Dearly beloved, we are gathered here in the sight of God and in the face of this company to join together this man and this woman in holy matrimony . . . . Into this holy estate these two persons present come now to be joined. If any man can show just cause why they may not lawfully be joined together, let him now speak . . . ."

Parishioner Carol Nielsen, donned in a tan dress trimmed with lace on the neck and three-quarter sleeves, glanced to the person to her right then to her left. Chin tilted upright, she locked her lips together before she stood up and opened her big mouth. Her large brimmed straw hat swayed on her head as she voiced her objection to the marriage. "I'm no man, but I'm going to state what's wrong with this wedding. Parson Quinn is a wealthy, upright minister, but he shouldn't marry widow Helen Gregory. She's poor and has all these children to take care, including Cliff and Billy. This will not work, and I'm speaking to head off the disaster that cometh."

Parson Adam's countenance turned red as he took a long breath before speaking. "Since you have no authority to interrupt this wedding, I must ask you to return to your seat, Mrs. Nielsen. Now we will continue with the vows." He glanced from the groom to the bride and smiled. "Do you wish to proceed?"

They both nodded in agreement.

Reverend Adam directed his attention to Pastor Quinn and said, "Wilt thou have this Woman to be thy wedded wife? Wilt thou love her, comfort her, honor and keep her in sickness and in health . . . so long as ye both shall live?"

Parson Quinn glanced at his wife to be. "I will."

Adam turned to Helen Gregory and stated, "Wilt thou have this Man to be thy wedded husband, to live together after God's ordinance in the holy estate of Matrimony. Wilt thou obey him and serve him, love, honor, and keep him in sickness and in health, keep thee only unto him, so long as ye both shall live?"

"I – I will," she replied in a soft tone then shifted her face from the minister to the man who stood beside her. She smiled at her husband to be.

Minister Adam presented the wedding ring and said, "With this ring, I thee wed, and with all my worldly goods, I thee endow. In the name of the Father, and of the Son, and of the Holy Ghost. Amen." Adam wove the couple's right hands together.

Quinn steadied his soon to be wife's shaking hand. *She's been through so much with the death of her husband and raising these young'uns. Lord, I ask for your blessing as we weave our families together.* He took a deep breath and gave her a small smile.

Adam continued with the ceremony. "Those whom God hath joined together let no man put asunder." He raised his head to those in attendance. "Forasmuch . . . in holy wedlock . . . I pronounce that they are man and wife . . . God the Father, bless, preserve, and keep you . . . that ye may so live together . . . have life everlasting. Amen."

Miss Pepperdine placed her hands on the organ's keys, and Cliff's deep voice rang out the third verse of the hymn, "Bless be the Tie That Binds." *We share our mutual woes, Our mutual burdens bear, And often for each other flows, The sympathizing tear.*

Quinn squeezed his wife's right hand then whispered into her ear. *The Lord has blessed our union, and even with the difficulties we face, our Lord is with us.*

Her hand shook slightly.

He tightened his grip and led her outside. *Smile, sweetheart, for be glad we found each other.*

She faced him and presented a nervous smile.

"Be confident. The Lord will provide our strength," he whispered into his wife's ear. The summer breeze brushed against their skins as Thomas Quinn and Helen stood outside to shake each attendee's hand. Only widow Carol Nielsen did not wish them well. Out of the corner of Quinn's eye, he observed the widow taking the reins of her buggy and leading her steeds homebound. *Good.* He hardened his clasp of his wife's hand. *What's wrong with that woman? She's one big troublemaker.*

* * *

Bonnets and Beaus, Book Four, *Faithful Vows*, is slated for release in 2025. For more information, visit: **http://authorJanetSyasNitsick.com**

Janet Syas Nitsick
Biography

Shy, natural redhead Janet Syas Nitsick's writing passion began as a child when she wrote a neighborhood play at 10-years-old. However, her dream of becoming a writer did not materialize until she became a journalist after earning her Bachelor of Arts degree from Omaha's College of Saint Mary in 1995 as a returning student.

Seasons of the Soul, her first book released in 2006, won Best of Year. In 2010 Janet's story, "The Silver Lining," placed 10th in the Writer's Digest mainstream/literary competition.

Janet writes mystery, suspenseful, clean, Christian, historical, homespun-romantic tales set in Nebraska. She is married and has four sons – two with autism. Her late father, Nebraska State Sen. George Syas, served 26 years in the Unicameral.

Janet's Web site: https://authorjanetsyasnitsick.com/
Janet's Blog: http://janetsyasnitsick.wordpress.com
Janet's Facebook Author Page:
https://www.facebook.com/authorjanetnitsick/

said. Oh, but that horse face of hers made Jim pine for his childhood nemesis, Annie Lee, who arrived in town a few weeks earlier.

He remembered the day he dipped his classmate's pigtails in the inkwell to repay her for breaking his slate. But now, despite his best efforts, he was falling in love with his former classmate and desired to court her instead of Betty.

However, he had to drop this wish when allegations of moral improprieties surfaced, which not only damaged his reputation but Annie Lee's as well. *The Bride List,* a humorous tale of a love-hate relationship that only the good Lord could ordain.

When Hearts Rekindle, third and last in Great Plains Series:

Thunderbolts echoed and rain pelted down as distraught Betty Chapman stood in agony to express her heartache from a broken courtship in Janet Syas Nitsick's new clean, historical romance, *When Hearts Rekindle.* This is her third and last book in the Great Plains Series.

To escape her pain, Betty travels from Elkhorn to Omaha, Neb., in 1894 to attend the Immanuel Lutheran Hospital Nursing School. While being escorted there during a blizzard, she and her driver become stuck and happen to arrive at the home of the Knudsons. This is where Betty meets Russ Knudson. He instantly takes stock of her familiarity to Gwen Ward, the beautiful woman he courted until she chose another. That similarity and the possibility of another heartbreak, Russ places distance between Betty and him.

However, Betty is not the only problem Russ faces. He and his father have secured a bank loan on the hope that their steer would win a blue ribbon at the upcoming county fair. Then they could sell that beef for a high price and pay off what they owed. But the banker wants Knudsons' land, and he and his cohorts will do everything to prevent them from doing so.

When Hearts Rekindle is a suspenseful, touching story about two lost souls searching for love but unable to embrace it, and a farm placed in jeopardy by the foolish actions of Russ and his father.

Visit Janet's Web site: https://authorjanetsyasnitsick.com or her blog **http://janetsyasnitsick.wordpress.com** for more information.

BONNETS & BEAUS SERIES

The Heiress Comes to Town, Bonnets & Beaus Series, Book One:

Slipping out of her father's New York mansion on her wedding day, Nina Robert stands outside her home in the snow to hail a cab. The cabbie pulls up just before her father would return in his rig with the minister.

She gets inside the cab, and the horses clomp to the train depot. With little money, she boards a train and eventually lands in Fort Calhoun, Nebraska.

There she hides out, gives a false name and meets Dr. Earl Olson, a young handsome doctor, who takes a liking to her. Love between them blossoms.

But her tycoon father, Clyde Robert the III, has not given up on finding her. To search for his daughter, Mr. Robert hires the famous Pinkerton National Detective Agency, known for their investigative work in foiling an assassination attempt on Abraham Lincoln's life during his first term. Nina's father also was determined to keep his daughter's arranged marriage to the wealthy son of a prominent and wealthy businessman intact.

Nina has settled into a happy, simple life working at the Greens Boardinghouse. Although poor, she is content in her escape haven, not under the dictates of a father who managed every move of her life. But once her father discovers her whereabouts, she faces another dilemma – stay and fight him or sneak away once again, either way she could lose the man she loves.

The Heiress Comes to Town, a clean, Christian historical romance, takes readers on a journey to small town life of 1896 before cars traveled the roadways and electricity illuminated buildings. Travel back in time and visit Nina's yearn for freedom and her desire to marry the man she loves.

The Librarian's Secret, Bonnets & Beaus Series, Book Two:

The library door creaked open. Footsteps approached. The elderly librarian glanced up as a man dressed in a hooded midnight-black cloak stopped in front of her and presented her his journal.

"... My confession is written in this journal."

Six years later, Heath Barrymore entered that same library to fulfill his deceased father's wishes – to discover where the librarian had placed the journal and expose the secret his father could not.

Heath stepped toward the librarian's desk, expecting to find gray-headed librarian Bessey, but instead his gaze met pretty Edna Hopper, the newly hired librarian who held a mysterious past.

Return to the 1890s in Nebraska City, Neb., and witness the love and heartache *The Librarian's Secret* presents to our hero and heroine, and what it holds for their futures.

Her Heart's Secret, Bonnets and Beaus, Book Three

As a child, Erina Higgins was surrounded by prestige and wealth. But that all changed when her family's scandal erupted, and the family was forced to move to the desolate prairie of Tekamah, Nebraska, in 1879.

Erina became a teacher and left Tekamah but returned after her mother passed away. There she reconnected with her childhood nemesis, Adam Miller.

Pastor Adam Miller was enchanted by Erina's fiery spirit, and there was no doubt in his mind that one day she would marry him.

Honey, you know we're meant for each other. Quit fighting what the Lord has ordained," said Adam Miller to skeptical Erina Higgins, who was determined not to wed him because that would disclose the family secret.

Visit Janet's Web site:
https://authorjanetsyasnitsick.com or her blog
http://janetsyasnitsick.wordpress.com for more information

PRAIRIE SISTERS SERIES

She Came by Train, Book One:

She Came by Train to leave behind her life of finery to travel to the Midwest to become a governess to two children of a widower businessman, Alex Boyer. Soon Alex and a preacher man, who hails from Virginia, the place of her origin, vie for her hand.

When the Whistle Blows, Book Two:

When the Whistle Blows takes readers to the Midwest of 1877, where two unlikely individuals collide with each other physically and emotionally. However, only Winifred can determine whether duty and Hugh's betrayal will keep her in Virginia or allow her to return to the man who still haunts her heart.

Visit Janet's Web site:
https://authorjanetsyasnitsick.com or her blog
http://janetsyasnitsick.wordpress.com for more information

STANDALONE CHRISTIAN ROMANCE

Her Husband's Secret (formerly published as Lockets and Lanterns):

As Edith marches down the aisle, she believes she is marrying the man of her dreams. But things are not always what they seem.

Her truthful, steadfast and faithful husband was hiding a secret – a secret so hurtful that bitterness consumed her. Can this fairytale marriage be saved for the sake of their children?

The answers dwell within her and through her Christian faith. *Her Husband's Secret* is a gripping tale of a shattered love, and the difficulty to forgive when trust breaks that marriage bond.

Visit Janet's Web site:
https://authorjanetsyasnitsick.com or her blog **http://janetsyasnitsick.wordpress.com** for more information.

SHORT STORIES AND PERSONAL ACCOUNTS

Seasons of the Soul, a book similar to Chicken Soup for the Soul books:

"Help!" said the eyes of my husband, Paul, as he stared glassy-eyed at me. He was submerged in the deep end of the hotel's swimming pool. Quickly, I swam over to him … to pull my oldest autistic son, Brad, off of him.

This begins one personal story presented in *Seasons of the Soul*, a 20-short-story collection written by Janet Syas Nitsick. Change is a fact of life, and that change is experienced through each person's own seasonal, spiritual journey. Janet and Paul's spiritual walk includes two autistic sons. *Seasons of the Soul*, an inspiration book of fictional, personal and children's stories, will make readers laugh, smile, cry and know God heals the hurting soul.

The Silver Lining:

This story received 10th place in the 79th Annual Writer's Digest Writing Competition in the mainstream/literary short story category. It is a bittersweet story of an elderly woman who remembers one afternoon with her daughter. People who enjoy Hans Christian Anderson's work, such as "The Steadfast Tin Soldier" and "The Little Match Girl," will love this touching story. It is a free read on Smashwords: https://www.smashwords.com/books/view/42833

Visit Janet's Web site: https://authorjanetsyasnitsick.com or her blog **http://janetsyasnitsick.wordpress.com** for more information.